WHAT OTHERS ARE SAYING:

"In a brilliant follow-up to his novel *'Cherries'*, John Podlaski weaves frightening events of his youth into a vivid depiction of a terrifying night as an infantryman on a Listening Post during the Vietnam War."
- Joe Campolo, Jr., Author of 'The Kansas NCO' and 'Back To the World.'

"What makes *When Can I Stop Running?* a different read from *Cherries* are the interludes where Polack's memories are brought to the surface as he warily watches for any movement near the LP, during which time he recalls his many adventures with school friends - some terrifying, some funny - while growing up in Detroit during the 1960's. It is in these stories - so familiar to those of us of the Boomer generation - that the author treats us to some of his finest writing. His childhood comes to life in his rich, poetic descriptions."
-Christopher Gaynor, newspaper journalist and author of 'A Soldier Boy Hears the Distant Guns'. Mr. Gaynor's work includes a feature story and photos in Time Magazine.

"Warrior and Vietnam author John Podlaski pulls out the stops in a very personal story interweaving some of his childhood experiences with his telling of his unnerving night spent in a listening post. A vividly written, yet tasteful, account of a nightmare experience...hair-raising and touching at the same time."
-William E. Peterson, International Best Selling and Award Winning Author: 'Missions of Fire And Mercy~Until Death Do Us Part' and 'Chopper Warriors~Kicking The Hornet's Nest'. Peterson's next work, coming in July 2016: 'Chopper Heroes.'

"John does a magical job in his second book of weaving the terrors of boyhood adventure with the terrors of war. His words had me laughing and crying while recalling and reliving some of my childhood adventures and the terror of pitch black nights alone on the floor of jungles of Vietnam. Thank you, John, for another great adventure!"

-Stephen Perry, Author of 'Bright Light: Untold Stories of the Top Secret War in Vietnam.'

"As I read, *'When Can I Stop Running'* and got deeper into the story, it brought all the images forward of those things I feared most – total darkness, rotting jungle, insects, and strange noises. I cringed at every turn, often asking myself if I had the bravado to do what they were doing. Today, soldiers use Night Vision Devices to see in the dark, quite a contrast from the Vietnam Era, when soldiers only had their hearing, sense of smell, and a vivid imagination to guide them in the pitch black jungle. I also appreciate the author's stories of his youth; the adventures are both frightening and funny, yet, I could relate to similar experiences while growing up. This book is the real deal! Great job, Mr. Podlaski!"

-R. Scott Ormond (Sgt-5 ReCon Scout and Tank Section 3d/33d Armor, Germany 1971-73)

WHEN CAN I STOP RUNNING?

WHEN CAN I STOP RUNNING?

By

JOHN PODLASKI

ISBN-13: 9781534775800
ISBN-10: 1546632158

Barbara Battestilli, Copy / Content Editor
Story Coordination by Janice J. Podlaski
Cover design by Nicole A. Patrick
Printed in the United States of America

While *'When Can I Stop Running?'* is largely a work of fiction, many of the events and anecdotes described in the book are from the actual experiences of the author. The places mentioned were real and did exist. All characters portrayed are fictional, and any resemblance to actual persons, living or dead, organizations, events, and locales, are entirely coincidental.

Acknowledgments:

I would like to thank all who have contributed to this work; your persistence, and faith in me kept my spirit alive. Special thanks to Barbara Battestilli, whose hard work, patience and great attention to detail polished my story and contributed to its readability. Finally, and most importantly, sincere thanks to my wife, Janice - without her love, sacrifices, and support over the years, this second work would not exist. I also want to recognize my pals, Paul and Wayne - you two made growing up a true adventure.

Dedication:

For Janice and Nicole – my loves forever!

God Bless America's soldiers – past, present, and future. Thank you for your service and my freedom!

Table of Contents

PREFACE

Have you ever been afraid? Truly afraid?

I'm talking about gut-wrenching fear - the kind you might experience when your very life is in danger. If so, chances are high that your feelings of terror occurred at night.

And why is night, in particular, the scariest part of the 24-hour day?

We all know that the dark of night can be daunting and may hide mysterious things. It's the time of day when sound carries, and a person may be unable to identify sudden strange noises, shifting shadows or other potential threats that may or may not be real. As a result, the imagination kicks in - supposedly to help the brain make decisions - but that just adds to the uncertainty and fear.

So what exactly is fear? The Dictionary defines it as, "an unpleasant emotion caused by the belief that someone or something is dangerous and likely to cause pain. A threat; something that causes feelings of dread or apprehension; the anticipation that something unpleasant will occur."

Impending danger, evil, pain - whether the threat is real or imagined - arouse this distressing emotion. Most of the time, what you don't see is more unnerving than what you do see.

Fear is a human adaptive response. It's normal and even helpful to experience fear in dangerous situations. It serves a protective purpose, activating the "fight-or-flight" response in all of us. Without fear, we'd jump headlong into things we shouldn't. With our bodies and minds alert and ready for action, we can respond quickly and protect ourselves.

Protect us from what? In most cases, the unknown!

Experiencing fear as children, the usual reaction was to call out to our parents for help. If they weren't around, then diving under a blanket or running away as fast as our legs could carry us seemed like the solution.

Of course, it's only natural that at that young age, certain events were terrifying to us. As adults, in retrospect, we may laugh at the memory of many of those things that frightened us when we were adolescents. However, other harrowing episodes may have left unhealed scars in our psyche, and looking back, they are not the least bit humorous to us.

For some, the very memory of being in hair-raising situations is nearly as traumatic as experiencing the actual event. Think about those men and women in the military who had deployed to a war zone, be it Vietnam, Iraq, Afghanistan, or anywhere else in the world. Step into their shoes for a moment and join them during a single patrol to seek out the enemy. It's like walking through a House of Horrors at a carnival. Everyone on the team expects something to happen at any moment. It might be an attack from an enemy soldier poised to kill you or a fellow infantryman, an unseen booby trap, or some other potentially fatal danger lurking around any corner. Fear is constantly present and running is not an option!

Bravery is the quality of spirit that enables you to face danger or pain, while conquering your fear. It demonstrates having the utmost confidence in your training. That is how many of us in the military survived.

'When Can I Stop Running?' is a story about fear and how the author ('Polack') dealt with it, both in Vietnam and throughout his childhood. Readers will accompany the author and his friend and fellow grunt ('LG') during a night-long mission in the jungles of Vietnam. The two lone soldiers are manning a "Listening Post," hiding in the dense shrubbery, some 500 meters outside the firebase perimeter. The author juxtaposes his nightmarish hours in the bush with some of his most heart-pounding childhood escapades. Readers may relate to the childish antics with amusement; military veterans will find themselves relating to both captivating collections.

"THE ONLY THING WE HAVE TO FEAR IS FEAR ITSELF"

FDR'S FIRST INAUGURAL ADDRESS

ONE - FIREBASE LYNCH & LISTENING POST

John Kowalski and Louis Gladwell (aka 'Polack' and 'LG') drew the short straws earlier that afternoon, which meant they would be spending the night by themselves in a Listening Post roughly 500 meters outside the wire – deep in the Iron Triangle jungles of Vietnam. In that morning's company briefing, First Squad of First Platoon was delegated to provide two warm bodies to man one of the four Listening Posts (LP's) for that night. As there were seven members in the squad, they elected to use varied lengths of straws; the shortest two drawn would get the "coveted" assignment – the assignment dreaded by all.

Four LP teams of two would be going out that night, each heading out on a compass azimuth to position themselves evenly around Firebase Lynch. Dubbed "human early warning systems" and "bait for the enemy," their job was only to hide, listen, and report any potential threats to the firebase. Polack and LG were assigned the approaches from the east. Ambush patrols were also leaving at the same time, but those squad-sized elements would be looking for a fight and would set up two clicks farther out. Two companies, Alpha and Charlie, were providing security for the forward artillery base and would remain on ready alert in the event of a ground attack on the base, or in case one of the ambush teams got into trouble.

Both soldiers were from the Detroit area; their homes were only four miles apart on the east side of the city. The two 'hometown boys' quickly discovered each other in the base and gave one another a complete run down of any news from their common neighborhood – an extremely welcome touch of home some thousands of miles away.

John was six feet tall, weighed 170 pounds, and was normally fair-complected, but the hot tropical sun had baked his skin to a dark bronze. He sported medium-brown hair, somewhat bleached out now, and a light mustache, both slightly longer than regulation. He'd been away from the main base camp and forward fire support bases for almost a month. Out in the jungles, personal grooming is way down on the list of daily priorities. There's no one to impress, and nobody cares how you look. His shaggy hair was definitely not an issue.

Louis stood a couple of inches taller, but his build was slightly on the lankier side than John's. He was African-American, with light, caramel-colored skin. His face was long and narrow, and his forehead and cheeks were lightly pitted with old scars. His frizzy black Afro was picked out a little more than three inches into a perfect circle surrounding his head. An olive drab-colored boony hat rested atop of his puff of hair, swaying and shimmying about, reacting to each movement. LG tried growing a goatee since arriving in-country but had only acquired a dozen or so half-inch long hairs that spread across his chin. He checked his hand mirror daily, anxious for any signs of goatee progress, not willing to give up the plan.

LG played basketball at Detroit's Pershing High School and was named to the "All-State" team during his final two

14

years. He carried a newspaper clipping detailing his success in his wallet and was extremely proud of that achievement. John also played basketball, but he had attended a Catholic high school with only two-hundred students. Both graduated in 1969, but never had a chance to play against one another because of the separation of leagues within the city. St. Thomas Apostle was a 'Class D' school due to its small size, and Pershing, a 'Class A' with over a thousand students. LG flunked some classes in his first semester at college and had his scholarship revoked; Uncle Sam was quick to find him afterward. Whenever Alpha Company spent a day or two in Cu Chi or one of these firebases, John and LG would both play basketball wherever they found a hoop mounted on a backboard. Pick-up games were always available but they never played on the same team. LG's team, always the dominant force, seldom lost a game.

Polack had arrived at the main base camp for the 25th Infantry Division in Cu Chi a month before LG – which meant he had experienced a full 30 more days of bunker guard, going out on patrols, and living through ambushes while humping through the jungle. You learned quickly in-county – there was no other choice – but time passed slowly, and a month of experience was worth a great deal there. Because he was grateful to his own mentors after his arrival at the camp, Polack was eager to help other 'Cherries' learn the ropes. LG – as irrepressible as he was – sensed Polack's sincerity, and appreciated his comraderie. LG had a quick smile, and a mischievous sense of humor. It wasn't long before the two became best buds. Although they were not in the same squad, both were part of the 1st platoon, 1st

15

Battalion, 27th Infantry Wolfhounds, which operated in the areas northwest of Saigon.

"Hey brother man," Polack called over to his partner, a smirk growing on his face, "you gonna tie down that boony hat?"

LG looked at Polack with an incredulous look on his face. Before he could respond, Polack added, "You do know that if you sneeze, or there's a sudden breeze, that hat's gonna take flight and fly with the wind."

LG suddenly realized the dig, rolled his eyes and shot Polack a one finger salute. "You know, man, I don't understand why I gotta wear this thing at all. It's fucking up my 'do!" LG reached up to ensure that his boony hat was still in place, and the ball of hair remained centered above his head.

"You're trippin, man! If you go out without a hat, you'll come back with a commune of bugs living in your hair. You should put it on the right way," Polack suggested.

"It ain't gonna happen, my brother. I sprayed bug juice in my hair - notice the sheen?" LG primped his hair again. "That should stop them bugs from getting in. Besides, I've worked too hard on this over the last week just to let it get fucked up on an overnight."

Polack laughed, "Don't forget that RTO's get picked off by snipers because of their antennae, which, by the way, are much shorter than you and your floating lid."

"Ha – Ha," LG mocked sarcastically, "It don't mean nothin'."

Just as LG finished his sentence, another shirtless African-American soldier arrived. His Afro hairstyle was identical to LG's, but instead of a hat, a long, black metal hair pick ("rake") stuck out from his ball of hair. It sat off to the side, and, worn like a tilted crown, reminded John of how Jughead wore his hat in the 'Archie' comic books. His skin color was like dark chocolate, and there was a twenty-inch braided black shoelace encircling his neck; a four-inch braided cross hung from the necklace and dangled over his chest. A similarly fashioned two-inch wide black bracelet ringed his right wrist. His boots were untied and unlaced from half of the eyelets; the laces tucked inside. *'Exceptionally casual today...he must think he's back home in Alabama,'* John thought.

The soldier wore a black leather holster on his right hip, the flap securing a military .45 caliber pistol. His jungle fatigues were worn, faded, and two sizes too big. James smiled and his perfect white teeth gleamed in the receding sunlight. A member of the First Platoon, he was a scrawny guy from Mobile and stood at least six inches shorter than the rest of his brethren in the platoon. As a result of his size, James often volunteered to check out enemy tunnels whenever the First Platoon uncovered them. As a tunnel rat, he'd soon find himself spending a lot of time underground after the Wolfhounds would discover dozens of tunnels and caches in this area during the coming months.

James and his squad spent the day humping through the jungle and turned up in the general area where Polack and LG were staying that night.

"Hey, Bloooooods," he called, dragging out the pronunciation of the second word in a long drawl. In his left hand, James held an ice-cold can of Coke, which sweated profusely in the humid air, moisture running down and dripping onto the ground. He moved in front of LG, held out his right fist waist-high between the two men, and then began a ritual handshake referred to as 'DAP.' Their hands moved up and down each other's arms, touching shoulders, snapping fingers, beating chests, slapping palms, bumping fists, and finally ending in a traditional brotherhood handshake.

"Y'all need to be careful out there tonight," he stated without missing a beat. "We saw beaucoup signs out on the trails today; a blind man could see that Charlie - and I mean lots of them - are out there just diddy-bopping along like they own the place." Finished with the greeting, James moved to Polack, and they began the ritual while he continued, "This be a bad mofo, my brothers, the smell of death is everywhere. Every hair on the back of my neck stood tall the whole time we humped today. There was also something in the air...hard to explain...a feeling! You know the one you get when you think somebody's laying back and watching you from the shadows?" Finishing his greeting, James stepped back a couple of paces.

Polack and LG both listened intently and could only shake their heads in affirmation while waiting for James to continue.

"Well, that's how it was, my brothers. We didn't see any of them today, but I do know for sure the man's out there, scoping us out and putting a plan together. You brothers keep your heads down and don't be no heroes out there." James raised the can of Coke and chugged it until empty.

"Damn, this shit is good! You want me to get y'all one?"

"No time, James, but thanks for the offer, brother," LG responded for the pair.

"Well, look here," James drawled, crushing the empty Coke can and tossing it into the nearby garbage barrel. "I just wanted to make sure I caught y'all before leaving so I could throw some luck your way! I'm hip about spending the night in the dark jungle, especially as part of an LP – I do know it can be a motherfucker! The beast is out there and will try to fuck with your head. Stay sharp, be strong, and don't let it in!"

Polack and LG smiled and chimed together in responding, "Thanks, brother man!"

"We'll be cool," Polack added.

"Well, alright then! See y'all in the morning." The three soldiers slapped low outstretched hands and James turned to leave. Before walking away, he looked up to LG's head,

"I like what you doin' with the new 'do, brother. Lookin' good!" The compliment resulted in an enormous smile from the tallest of the trio. "But that hat got to go, my man!" LG's smile quickly disappeared, replaced by the frown he'd worn earlier. James raised his right fist and softly beat it against his chest once then walked away toward the mess tent shaking his head back and forth in amusement.

The two men returned the salute and then turned to one another.

"So what you think, Polack?"

"About what? Your hat?"

"Naw, man! Fuck the hat!" LG kicked at the ground in retaliation, his toe upending a divot of dirt that sailed toward his partner, found its mark, and covered his boots in a shower of red dust.

Polack jumped in surprise. "What the…?" he started to say in annoyance, but stopped when he saw LG's wide grin. Both men burst out laughing and after a few seconds slapped hands before resuming gathering their supplies.

LG was first to speak up,

"Come on, bro, let's be serious here." The tall man spread out his hands, palms up, in a pleading gesture.

Polack's demeanor changed.

"Okay, okay! Lay it on me," Polack conceded, tucking his hands into the back pockets of his trousers and appearing more attentive.

Polack couldn't help but notice that the scene surrounding the two men was a beehive of activity. Dusk was only thirty minutes away, and troops across the firebase were scrambling to prepare for the coming night. Artillery crews worked on the battery of six Howitzers. Men were busy removing 105 mm rounds from storage containers and tossing the empty wooden crates onto the other side of the wall of sandbags surrounding the guns. In the morning, a work detail would fill these with dirt and use them to build living quarters for others on the firebase.

The teams leaving the firebase at night would travel lightly without the extra weight of rucksacks, helmets, and food. Each man would carry only the bare necessities: weapons, extra ammo, trip flares, claymore mines, grenades, camouflaged poncho liners tied to the back of their web gear, and one PRC-25 radio per group. The heat and humidity took a toll on everyone during the day, but the nights were extremely chilly and damp. Poncho liners kept them warm; soldiers cocooned themselves, using the liners as shields against the jungle bugs – especially the swarms of mosquitoes. All four ambush squads carried an M-60 machine gun and extra belts of ammo; each member also had a single belt of 100 rounds to support the gun.

Scanning the camp, Polack noticed individual groups of four soldiers strolling toward the eight perimeter bunkers. Weapons and web gear hung limply from their shoulders; lightweight poncho liners poked out from under arms, some rolled and others just gathered up into a ball. Most carried a single green sock in one hand, usually filled with C-Ration canned desserts such as peaches, apricots, pound cake, or pecan rolls – popular treats, but difficult to obtain. Those highly-prized items were frequently used in bartering with others for something the men might need to help get them through the long, boring night: books, magazines, letters or writing materials, which stuck out of pockets all around. Most soldiers hoped to read and write what they could before it became too dark to see. Troops tossed empty soda cans into nearby trash barrels in passing and shared laughs among themselves en route. They pulled guard duty in the bunkers from 1800 hours until 0600 hours – two men on, and two sleeping, switching every two hours.

Farther away, other foursomes played "grabass" and horsed around, tossing pebbles at one another, then snatching each other's boony hats while playing "keep away": a single moment of innocence and an opportunity to act like other boys their age back home.

Before long, it's shift-change on the bunker line and time to relieve the two soldiers who've been there since daybreak. They'll be given just enough time to catch a meal

21

at the mess tent, and then relax a bit in a square, makeshift structure fabricated from artillery wooden crates, perforated metal planks (PSP), dirt, and sandbags. Each of those windowless units was large enough to provide shade and shelter for a squad of soldiers sleeping in hammocks. Fortunately, they were newly constructed, and rats hadn't had a chance to move in yet. Sleep would come easy for them until the scavengers invaded!

"I'm talking about what James said about all the gooks out there," LG ranted, breaking through Polack's observations. "It's going to be bad enough out there in the pitch black jungle with us having to fight bugs and creatures, and lay there and smell that rotten, dying shit because of that damn weed killer they sprayed all over, and now we gotta worry about gooks sneaking up on us this close to the firebase."

"Relax, G. Tonight won't be any different than all the other times we pulled LP or went out on night ambushes. Nothing has changed, my man."

"Yeah, but this is the Triangle, bro. The area's got a rep, and folks sayin' there's nothin' but gooks and death everywhere."

"So it's got a rep - big deal," Polack looked directly into LG's brown eyes. "We've been in places just as bad, if not worse." LG's eyes glinted; a questioning look crossing his face. Polack continued, "Did the Hobo Woods have a rep?"

"Yeah," LG mumbled.

"What about the Michelin Rubber Plantation?"

"Yep."

"Xuan Loc?"

"Okay, okay, I get it!" the gangly soldier groaned. "All of the 'Nam has a rep."

"And we're still here, right?"

"You right, my brother," LG acknowledged, "but tonight just feels different to me." LG looked at the ground, awaiting encouragement.

"It should feel different." Polack emphasized. "This is a new place for us, and it's the first time we're going outside the wire. Neither one of us knows what's out there. The unknown will try to fuck with us tonight. I know it can be a bitch. Just don't freak out on me, G!"

LG looked at his partner. "You mean to tell me that this shit don't bother you?"

"I didn't say that, bro. I hate the night. Always did! The night scares me more than the gooks," Polack hesitated for a moment, trying to vanquish the disturbing sensation he felt. LG stood in place, wide-eyed, listening intently and looking stunned. "I do feel better knowing that you'll be out there with me, G. And tonight, we only have to hide and listen. We'll be invisible, and the Beast won't find us. Let it go, brother!"

LG looked relieved. "Yeah, you right, we've got each other's backs. Fuck the Beast!"

The two men slapped hands again.

Polack looked toward the main gate and noted that the rest of his group was painting up. "We need to finish up here and head over to Rock's squad for our final check."

LG glanced over to the gate and rolled his eyes, "It's time for make-up." He stepped in front of Polack with two camouflage sticks, immediately rubbing alternating black and green stripes on his friend's face and hands. When no

23

more white skin was showing, a satisfied LG handed the sticks to Polack and waited for him to reciprocate. "Now we almost the same color, brother!", he grinned.

The PRC-25 radio attached onto an aluminum frame with a "quick drop" harness. When engaged, it allowed the RTO to dump his rucksack quickly in the event of an ambush or some other emergency. That night, however, LG left the frame behind and instead connected a strap to the 26-pound radio, letting it hang from his right shoulder. To balance the weight, a canvas bag filled with baseball grenades and two claymore mines hung heavily from his left shoulder. Polack carried a canvas bag on each shoulder, both filled with flares, grenades, one claymore mine and smoke grenades.

LG snatched his rifle from the wall of sandbags and held it by the handle in his right hand.

"You ready for this?" he asked.

"Let's do it!" Polack shot back.

They walked to the gate and got into line with the nine other soldiers in Sgt. Rock's squad. The non-commissioned officer wore a holster bearing a .45 caliber pistol on his hip and completed a personal inspection of each man in the line. When he came to LG, the esteemed NCO quickly reached up with both hands and snatched the sides of LG's boony hat, forcefully yanking it down hard. The brim bottomed out on the man's ears; the crown strained to fit over the thick puff of hair, forcing clumps of unruly frizz to poke out comically from the sides. LG was stunned and stood with his mouth agape, mollified and speechless.

"This isn't the time to make a fashion statement, LG!" Sgt. Rock snarled. He folded his muscular arms across his barrel chest, backed up a step and glared into the tall soldier's eyes, soliciting snickers from the line of soldiers.

LG, embarrassed now, decided to leave his hat right where it was. He looked down and stammered meekly, "Sorry, Rock!"

Rock pursed his lips and nodded to the man,

"Don't do that again, troop!"

When Rock walked away, Polack couldn't resist and stifled a chuckle.

"Don't say I didn't warn ya, bud!"

LG could only scowl at his partner, still taken aback at what had just happened.

Sgt. Rock spread a map out on the ground.

"Okay guys, gather around and listen up."

Firebase Lynch stood on a patch of land not far from the city of Xuan Loc and within the footprint of an area identified as the Iron Triangle. Three lines were drawn on a map outlining the 125 square miles of thick forests and rubber trees. The three points of the triangle connected the towns of Ben Cat, Ben Suc, and Phu Hoa. The Boi Loi and Hobo Woods bordered the Triangle along one side and the Fil Hol and Michelin Rubber Plantation on the other. The Iron Triangle was known to be an enemy stronghold filled with miles of tunnels, underground hospitals, training centers, base camps and rest points dating back to before World War II. In the early part of the war, American and Army of the Republic of Vietnam (ARVN) forces destroyed most of the villages in the Triangle and relocated those families to new facilities in a different area of the country. Much of the Triangle became a "free fire zone" meaning that curfews didn't apply and anyone out and about was considered the enemy - soldiers were expected to shoot there first without requiring clearance. Those remaining villages on the outskirts of the Triangle were extremely supportive of both the Viet Cong (VC) and North Vietnamese Army (NVA) troops, making the fight to drive out the enemy almost impossible. The Triangle was always a major gateway between the infamous Ho Chi Minh trail in Cambodia and Saigon, the capital of South Vietnam.

The Iron Triangle had lost much of its concealment over time, a result of the U.S. military spraying a defoliant called "Agent Orange" throughout the zone. A majority of the foliage had since rotted and decayed, leaving swatches of thinned out and barren earth in its wake. All the porous tree stumps became havens for red ants, spiders, horseflies, and other crawling insects, which feasted on the rotting vegetation. Red ants stung unmercifully; horseflies left painful welts after biting their victims, and a hundred different varieties of spiders sent chills down the spines of young soldiers from both sides.

However, a large portion of the jungle within the Triangle remained intact and continued to provide concealment for hundreds of active infiltration routes. The U.S. Army deemed it necessary to build a firebase and inserted the 1st Battalion Wolfhounds of the 25th Infantry Division into this quagmire to once again try to stop the flow of fresh enemy troops and supplies.

During the previous few days, recon patrols operating around the firebase had located different trails, all showing recent heavy activity, and some were within a couple of clicks of the firebase. The battalion leadership, concerned about their proximity, concentrated their efforts on these trails and kept squad-sized units patrolling within four clicks of the wire. Colonel Smith and his staff identified primary and secondary ambush locations and places where the LP's could hole up each night. During the briefing two hours earlier, squad leaders were given small topographical maps of the area; routes were identified and final destinations circled with a red grease pencil. Team leaders would conduct final briefings with their teams just before departure, which is what Sgt. Rock was doing at the moment. He went over the assigned primary and alternate bush locations, radio call signs, and had the men conduct a weapons check. Just before leaving, Rock conducted another physical inspection of each squad member to ensure shirt sleeves were down completely, all exposed skin was covered with camouflage paint, all specified supplies were available, and finally, that nothing rattled. Afterward, the men hurriedly took last drags of their cigarettes before stomping the butts into the earth. Once outside of the firebase, there was no smoking, talking or eating until their return the following morning.

Rock led his squad through the gate, leaving the relative safety of the firebase. The engineers had plowed back the jungle 200 meters beyond the wire, providing those guards on the perimeter an unobstructed view to open fields of fire to repel enemy ground attacks. However, the ground was uneven and covered with large, deep tracks from the heavy equipment. Exposed tree roots, pieces of tree bark, branches and bowling ball-sized chunks of clay added to the obstacle course, making the march in the twilight hazardous for the single file of eleven soldiers. The point man followed a compass azimuth of 90 degrees (due east) leading into the jungle. Once they entered, most of the light disappeared, forcing the line of soldiers to tighten up their distance between one another and not lose sight of the man in front of him. After advancing along the trail for about ten minutes, Sgt. Rock stopped the squad when they came upon an intersecting path, then touched Polack and LG on the shoulder, and pointed silently to a clump of bushes about twenty feet to their left. The two men stepped out of line; the remaining soldiers began moving again, each man offering either a thumbs-up or a peace sign to the two soldiers as they passed. Within seconds, they had vanished into the darkness.

Polack led the way down the trail, moving twenty paces before stepping off and breaking a path through the chosen clump of thick brush until reaching a small hollowed out depression twenty more paces above the trail. This was a great spot for the night listening post. Two small trees, only inches apart, stretched up from the ground at the rear of the eight-foot diameter depression, their trunks, as thick as Polack's thigh, would provide adequate back support for both men. Their position was encircled by thick, thorny brush, hanging vines, and other seemingly impenetrable jungle vegetation. One hundred feet overhead, the jungle canopy swayed gently in the breeze, releasing leaves to fall and gather on the damp ground.

Polack looked inquisitively at LG, awaiting his concurrence. LG quickly scanned the area and gave his approval by raising his right hand and giving Polack the "OK" sign.

With visibility at just ten feet, both men had to hustle and ready their position before it was too dark to see.

Polack took the radio, placed it between the two trees, then double-checked the frequency. Finding the dials locked in the correct positions, he snatched up the handset, depressed the button on the side, and whispered into the mouthpiece, "Thunder 3, this is Lima Papa 1. Radio check, over."

"This is Thunder 3, we have you, Lima Charlie, how me? Over," a monotone voice responded, informing him that the transmission was heard "loud and clear" on the other end. The volume was somewhat blaring and metallic in his ear, but Polack recognized the voice belonging to Red, a member of the Alpha Company CP.

Smiling, he quickly turned down the volume and responded, "This is Lima Papa 1, have you same-same. Be advised we are in our designated position, over," Polack answered quietly.

"Roger Lima Papa 1, stay safe, out."

While Polack conducted the radio check, LG crawled out and positioned his two claymore mines so one pointed toward the large trail and the other to their front. He fed the wires back through the brush, plugged the ends into a clacker (arming device), and set them on the ground in front of the radio. After the commo check, Polack quickly crawled out diagonally to his left about thirty feet and positioned his claymore mine to cover the left approach of the trail. He returned after two minutes, armed his mine, then laid the trigger next to the other two. The three firing devices lay on the ground side by side, pointing in the direction covered by each mine. In the event that their position became compromised from one of those directions, the correct device was readily available and could be fired within seconds. The last thing they did in the quickly fading twilight was to straighten the safety pins on their grenades and place them in a row in front of the claymore devices.

In this LP, both men understood their assignment: sit, listen and report any enemy movement during the night. Firing a weapon in the darkness would immediately expose their position, enabling the enemy to find and kill them. The mines and grenades offered a line of defense without giving away their position. If discovered, both men were to take whatever action necessary to protect themselves and evade the enemy while attempting to return to the firebase.

Polack and LG sat in the depression and used the two trees for back rests, the radio and armaments were in place on the ground and within reach between them. Trying to get comfortable, both men happened to catch each others eyes, barely visible in the darkness. LG offered a weak smile of confidence which Polack quickly returned. Both bumped fists in a mini-DAP and settled in for the long night.

Polack picked up the radio handset, cradled it on his shoulder, and then tapped LG to get his attention. Seeing only the whites of his eyes, Polack pointed to himself then to the luminous dial on his watch, and held up two fingers close to LG's face, hoping LG was able to see them. LG responded with the "OK" sign, equally close to Polack's face, then covered himself with his poncho liner, understanding that Polack was taking the first watch and would wake him in two hours.

At not yet seven in the evening, the light of the crescent moon wasn't bright enough to penetrate the thick foliage. Soon it was so dark that Polack was unable to see his own hand moving only inches in front of his face. He blinked a few times just to verify that his eyes were open. It was no use; whether they were open or closed, he could see nothing.

As the nocturnal creatures woke, the cacophony of their various sounds carried through the darkness. This symphony was sure to grow louder as the night progressed. Right then, it was calming in a way, and one could imagine that all the individual mating calls were timed and repeated in a closed loop. If the noise stopped, then it was time to worry.

Polack hated the dark, especially when it was like this. Everything was shaded either dark gray or ink black without a sign of color anywhere. With eyes opened or closed, it was all the same, and he felt as claustrophobic as if sitting in a small closet in the middle of the night. In addition, the rotting smell of dead vegetation as a result of the defoliant Agent Orange made him nauseous. His hearing now enhanced, his mind actively tried to absorb all the sounds, applying filters to help recognize those which did not belong. Adrenaline was ready to soar - just waiting for the right signal.

LG's breathing settled into a steady rhythm, making it clear that he was sound asleep. Without any visual stimuli to keep his mind occupied, it had a tendency to wander, and in this case, caused Polack to get lost in his thoughts. A memory jumped out, sending him back to the age of seven.

TWO - THE BASEMENT

Let's face it, darkness can be scary. Being in the dark can sometimes give you the unnerving feeling that you are being watched. Children everywhere may feel nervous about closets and the "spooky" space under their beds, but while those patches of darkness can be intimidating for some, for me, there was a much creepier place: our basement. Built in the 1930's, our house in Detroit had an unfinished basement typical of most in the neighborhood, and its basement was dark and cellar-like. When my parents sent any of us kids downstairs on an errand after dark, it was considered a sure death sentence.

Early one day, at the tender age of seven, I accompanied my mother into the basement when it was time to change loads in the washing machine. Although shafts of sunlight glared brightly through the high window panes, she did turn on the light over our old wringer-style washing machine. Nevertheless, I followed right on her heels, making sure that I stayed close, and that I kept her in between me and that monstrous old furnace.

I watched Mom as she pulled an article of sopping wet clothing from the barrel of the washing machine and fed it cautiously into the mouth of two horizontal rollers just above the basin. Clothes were crushed by this powerful squeezing process resulting in a steady stream of water that fell into a nearby washtub. A wild whirlpool of water spun over the drain in the center until the last item of clothing fell into the basket with a thud.

Why is it that when somebody tells a child that he or she shouldn't do something, it seems more like a dare? While Mom continued to feed articles of clothing through the crusher, she cautioned me, "Be very careful of these rollers. They'll catch your fingers and crush them if you're not paying attention!" (Note to self: "Investigate that roller thingy when I get a chance.")

While Mom was busy with the laundry, I used the time to study my surroundings. Several four-inch wide cast iron poles stood like sentinels every ten feet. Old furniture, stored haphazardly on the floor and draped with white bed sheets looked eerie, even during the day. Wooden boxes contained tools and other miscellaneous junk. Dozens of them were stacked adjacent to the ghostly-looking furniture that ran the length of the remaining wall. Then, of course, the huge, ugly furnace - looking like a torture chamber from the Dark Ages - took up much of the floor space near the rear corner.

Our basement lighting was sparse and comprised of just a few lights strategically placed on the ceiling. Every light had a pull-cord or chain attached to turn it on and off. A bare light bulb above the washing machine hung from the end of a foot-long electrical cord and swayed back and forth, casting animated waves of light into the shadows, worsening any sense of foreboding that already existed.

Three small storage rooms lined the far end of the basement. I wasn't sure if the homemade plywood doors were meant to keep the things inside hidden from strangers, or to keep the things inside from getting out. The left-most room stored coal and kindling wood for the winter. The middle room was full of Christmas ornaments, Halloween decorations and out-of-season clothing, which hung from hangers on a horizontal metal pipe. The far right room was a pantry filled with dozens of home-canned glass jars of vegetables and fruits stored on shelves, and boxes filled with empty extra jars, lids and screw-on rings. I should also mention that the pantry door was in the corner behind the behemoth furnace.

It was time well spent, as I was able to plot a mental route from the stairway to the storage rooms at the far end of the dungeon-like setting. I felt the need to have a plan, just in case I ever had to come down here alone, which by the way, happened later that night.

After dinner, while Mom was busy washing dishes, she asked me to run down to the basement and bring up her short, brown winter jacket with the fur collar from the center storage room. She mentioned that the weather had turned chilly and that she would need it to wear to church the following morning. I stood there for a moment, stunned, and thinking hard for a way to get out of it! I was pretty sure that something evil lived behind each of the doors down there, waiting patiently in the pitch darkness for some unsuspecting schmuck like me to let it out. I was extremely anxious and felt veritably rooted to the kitchen floor.

My mother, seeing my apprehension, usually had to prod me (and sometimes threaten me) to get me moving. I remember her exasperation, finally warning me: "There's nothing down there that can hurt you. Get moving before I lock you down there for good!" My father's voice then boomed from the living room, "Johnny, be a man!" Hell, I was only seven years old and far from being a man, but I couldn't let my father down. There was no way out of this; I had to do it!

The dim lightbulb at the top of the stairs provided just enough artificial light to expose the stairway and cinderblock wall beyond the final step. I remember venturing down the staircase ever so slowly, keeping my eyes focused on the darkness ahead and then taking a break to catch my breath on the bottom step.

I stood perfectly still, staring intently into the darkness, contemplating my next move. A chill suddenly ran down my spine when I heard a creak near the furnace. I was positive something evil was hiding in the shadows behind the old coal burner, patiently waiting for me to move forward into the darkness. My racing heart caused beads of sweat to gather on my forehead, a single drop broke away and found its way into my right eye. My vision blurred and I began to panic. The last thing I wanted to do was close my eyes until the sweat washed away, and I could see again. That was not an option, as the monsters would be all over me within seconds. I quickly wiped my eye and forehead with my shirt sleeve, ready to bolt at the first sign of the slightest movement.

My route and timing had to be spot-on through this obstacle course, or I'd end up lost in the dark and probably die within 30 seconds. Ready or not, it was time to go!

I took one last deep breath and then leaped into the darkness, jumping up to reach the pull chains of every light as quickly as possible to keep the hidden monsters at bay. Finally, I was standing at door number two.

I don't care how many times I performed this task - the process never changed. The doors all opened outward and had small handles positioned on the left side, hinges on the right. Moving to my left a few steps, I'd hold my breath and approach the door from an angle, shuffling my feet only inches at a time. I made sure to keep my body clear of the door's swinging path in the event that somebody hiding inside tried to use a battering ram. Once there, I'd slide my right foot forward and jam it into the small gap at the bottom of the door. With shaking hands, I unhooked the latch. I had a rule about waiting a full five seconds to be sure that nothing tried to force its way out; then I'd swing the door open completely. Stale and musty odors permeated through the open doorway - nothing vile there, just typical old, unfinished basement smells.

The next element in this challenge was for me to step slowly into the darkness and locate the hanging light in the center of the eight by eight-foot room. I'd raise my arms and wave them in front of my face, taking small baby steps, until finally snagging the chain from the hanging light and quickly pulling it down to light up the room.

That evening, I lucked out and immediately spotted Mom's jacket on the overhead bar. Once I had it in hand, I had to execute my escape plan from this nightmarish place. Taking a few deep breaths in and exhaling out of my mouth slowly, I yanked down on the light chain and jumped free of the room. Slamming the door, I leaned against it to prevent whatever might have been hiding in the shadows from getting out and grabbing me. All that remained was for me to lock the door and hightail it out of there. After re-hooking the door, I placed my foot at the base of the plywood door and prepared myself as a runner might in starting blocks.

After hearing a silent signal in my head, I launched myself across the length of the basement, pulling down on every light chain while aiming for the stairs. Once there, I charged up the steps, two at a time, and jumped headfirst through the open doorway, landing hard on the kitchen floor. My foot automatically pushed out and caught the edge of the wooden door behind me, sending it on its arc at a speed slightly less than sound. The metal hinges screeched briefly in protest before a deafening slam, announcing the journey's end, and startling everyone in the house. Reaching up, I engaged the latch. Start to finish, the entire process took less than five minutes.

My mission into Hell was a success and I could now take a deep breath to celebrate. My feeling of self-gratification, however, was soon interrupted by Mom. She proceeded to scold me for making such a production out of a simple trip to the basement, citing that the sudden banging noise had stopped her heart. 'If she only knew,' I thought.

Of course, my fear of our basement diminished when I got older. When I was 12 years old, my father properly introduced me to the furnace. He taught me how to stoke a fire, add coal, and remove ashes through the heavy iron door at the bottom of the huge furnace. It still looked like a giant octopus hung upside down from the ceiling with tentacles (the round circular duct work) jutting out in all directions. It became my job to check the fire before and after school. It wasn't long before I was assigned the full-time responsibility of maintaining the furnace during the winter months, occasionally requiring visits in the middle of the night to get the fire going again. This job continued for the next couple of years until my parents saved enough money to purchase a new furnace. Thankfully, they converted to gas heat.

Later, when I discovered an interest in girls, the basement became my friend. I found a used couch and television set at the local Salvation Army and set up a small area to socialize with friends of both genders. At times, one or more of us spent the night amongst the shadows, not worried in the least.

As I got older, I do remember occasionally asking my younger sister or brother to fetch something from the basement for me. It was like asking them to descend into a crypt! Neither of them would go. Instead they would suddenly become "busy" or would disappear into their rooms, leaving me to retrieve the article myself. I became irritated with their attitude...until I remembered my own past fear of the shadows and unknown creatures lurking below!

THREE - LISTENING POST (2000 HOURS)

Polack's memories were suddenly interrupted when the steady rush of white noise on the radio handset disappeared. After several seconds, a voice whispered in his ear, "Lima Papa 1, Thunder 3, sit-rep, over." Polack hadn't heard anything out of the ordinary or seen anything beyond the end of his nose, so he depressed the talk button on the handset, holding it down for a split second, indicating an 'all clear' status. When he let up, the static returned briefly before the voice whispered in acknowledgment, "Roger, 1." The battalion radio operator then continued his query of the other units in the jungle; all responded with a single break in the squelch. When finished, the white noise returned to keep Polack company for another hour.

If any of the elements felt threatened or suspected enemy forces nearby, the radio operator would respond with two quick breaks in the squelch instead of a single one. When that happened, the battalion RTO immediately announced on the frequency, "Check, check, check. This is Thunder 3 - hold your traffic on this net and keep it open unless there is an emergency. Out." That response quickly garnered the attention of everyone listening in on the frequency, including members of the battalion Command Platoon. They'd all stand-by and wait in nervous anticipation for the next update from the unit in distress.

Polack was placed on LP twice before since arriving in country, however, neither of the former assignments were in jungle as dense as this. His first was actually inside of Cu Chi base camp during in-country training, delegated to an obscure location within the wire and facing the village of Cu Chi. His job that night was to watch for sappers in the wire and villagers moving about during the curfew. There was so much illumination from the base camp throughout the night that his position was as brightly lit as late afternoon. That particular location was probably the most secure of any within the country. Nevertheless, Polack felt anxious and insecure sitting there alone on only his fifth day in-country. His second turn at LP was during a week-long, platoon-sized patrol through the Michelin Rubber Plantation. There, he and another squad member spent the night lying on their bellies 200 feet outside their night defensive perimeter. With hardly any vegetation to cast shadows or hide behind, the full moon lit up the area like a night baseball game at Tiger Stadium. They'd lay in the shadows of seedling trees, shifting positions regularly to stay within the small trees' silhouettes as the moon crossed the sky. They could see in any direction for at least a mile, and help - in the event that it was needed - was only seconds away.

Polack and LG both earned their Combat Infantryman Badge (CIB's) many times over while patrolling through the jungle with their platoon. However, no matter how much experience a person had, a night in a two-man outpost in known enemy territory during the pitch blackness of night took a toll on its occupants both physically and mentally. These men were well-trained soldiers, taught how to react in any situation. They practiced every scenario and had the right procedures drummed into their heads repeatedly over the past several months. The correct response should be immediate, with the body operating on autopilot. Fear caused panic, which interfered with a soldier's ability to follow protocol and react per his training. It was also a sure fire way to get yourself killed!

Their latest LP position was set up within a large thicket of vegetation, making physical movement both difficult and restricted. Sitting on the hard ground for extended periods of time put John's ass to sleep – not only figuratively, but by numbing and cramping his backside and legs. It was impossible to stand up in these locations to stretch or to move about without making lots of noise, thereby exposing their position. Sound carried at night through the jungle and those nearby quickly reacted to it.

Finding a comfortable body position for the night was paramount. It was also important to protect your eyes from getting poked by the thickets of twigs and branches surrounding them. Joint and body stiffness was guaranteed in the morning after sleeping on the hard, uneven ground. Soldiers took their time when returning to the firebase, using the short hump as a way to work out their kinks and stretch out the soreness. If it became necessary for the two men to bug out because of enemy pressure during the night, stiffness impeded a fast getaway, and would not serve them well.

Fighting mosquitoes, fire ants, snakes, spiders, centipedes, and horseflies was a battle in itself. Army-issued insect repellent ("bug juice") helped to keep many of the mosquitoes at bay, but the relief seemed to last just a couple of hours or so. The need to reapply the liquid by hand at every opportunity was a necessary effort to keep mosquitoes away during the long night. Wrapping oneself inside a poncho liner offered some protection from the biting insects but the constant drone of those flying swarms was nerve-wracking, and the continuous buzzing around their ears kept the men awake for the duration.

Red ants were also relentless when attacking; their bites felt like burning cigarettes against the skin. These communal insects are territorial, and they will drop on you from overhead tree leaves or attack you from the ground if you threaten their domain. Swatting the air and continuously wiping off your clothes in the bush might keep some bugs away, but it might also be your fatal mistake, divulging your position to those on the look out.

You can't see snakes, spiders, and centipedes crawling around in the black of night, so there was no sense worrying about them, unless, of course, they landed or crawled over the men's bodies. When that happened, it took all the fortitude they could muster to contain a blood curdling scream and stop themselves from unassing the area. Of course, there were no lights available to turn on and investigate; flashlights and lighters were prohibited. Light is visible at great distances during the night and serves as a beacon, letting the enemy know your whereabouts.

Imagine sitting in total darkness and being unable to see anything at all. It's a form of sensory deprivation; your imagination switches into overdrive and provides images of what it thinks might be out there. Paranoia takes over and the mind begins to think of doomsday scenarios. Panic strikes and the adrenaline starts pumping quickly through the body, preparing it to fight or run. Running away had always worked when younger, and survival then was pretty much a given. However, in war, that's not an option. The men had to depend on their training, and instead, face their fears or die.

It was still quiet around the position, and Polack had no reason for concern. Soon, he'd be able to get some shut-eye after he woke LG to take over the watch at 2100 hours. The jungle tedium once again took hold of Polack, his mind slowly pulling him back to memories of his childhood

FOUR - SUMMER CAMP

I spent most of my early years going to annual summer camp, joining other boys aged 8 to 15 from the inner city of Detroit. We shared a three-hour bus ride up Gratiot Avenue to our destination, a few miles north of Lexington, Michigan. The camp was situated on the shores of Lake Huron, one of Michigan's spectacular Great Lakes. There, I learned to swim, canoe, fish, shoot arrows at targets, braid colored plastic strips into lanyards and whips, draw, paint, and play baseball, basketball, and touch football. It was also there that I endured some of my most vividly frightening childhood experiences.

The camp, bordered by forest on three sides, contained spruce, pine, fir, oak, maple and birch trees. They rose up from the ground in no particular track or pattern, almost as if handfuls of seed were scattered to the winds centuries ago. Scrub brush, weeds, vines, and other ground-cover grew thickly between the trees, using the trunks as trusses to rise high and dense, and seemed impenetrable.

The camp proper was almost a quarter-mile into the towering hardwoods and was invisible from the main highway. A narrow road cutting through the trees was the only telltale sign of its existence. Blink while driving by at 55 mph, and you'd miss it. The asphalt-covered roadway snaked through the thick forest, just wide enough to accommodate the five buses filled with campers.

The buses had to bulldoze their way through the canopy, and, once encapsulated, the interior darkened as green leaf-filled branches smothered them. The foliage scraped against windows on both sides of the bus, resulting in an eerie high-pitched squeal. Some of the young city kids began to panic, as they had never witnessed anything like that before. Those who had been there before consoled those who needed it. After what seemed like an hour of traveling through the dark tunnel of trees - but in reality was a mere several minutes - we exited into a spacious clearing dominated by a colossal log structure. The buses followed the circular drive and came to a stop in front of the massive building, which housed the business office, infirmary, kitchen, dining hall and activity center. A welcoming committee gathered in front, shouting words of welcome and encouragement while helping us out of the buses and cross-checking names against a roster. Once everyone was present and accounted for, three-hundred anxious boys and five hungry bus drivers went inside for lunch.

The traditional tour of the camp took place next, during which the counselors proudly pointed out any renovations completed since the previous summer. As they passed through the recreation area, repeat-campers excitedly called out to friends they hadn't seen for the entire school year, while the newbies took in all of the playground equipment in wide-eyed awe.

Directly behind the large building, the grounds encompassed an open area roughly a half-mile by a quarter-mile. The northern and southern boundaries were marked by dense tree lines, extending out to the rocky shoreline of

Lake Huron. The camp proper included two baseball diamonds with bleachers, an oval four-lane dirt running track circling both ball fields, and two volleyball courts outlined on a section of tan-colored sand. A large slab of black asphalt was home to the camp's basketball court; eight rims mounted to wood backboards atop ten-foot tall black iron poles sat idly, awaiting pickup games. Six hay bales were positioned on the ground along the tree line on the south side near the beach; a cardboard target hung from the face of each stack.

Fifteen small log cabins lined the northern tree line, and each was home to twenty campers. The buildings were separated by large plots of barren brown earth, dotted with green weeds and yellow dandelions. Four similar structures - showers and toilet facilities - were strategically positioned to their front about 50 yards away.

On the lake, a wooden dock extended thirty-five feet into the water, affording campers and staff an opportunity to jump or dive into the deep, rolling waves. On the beach, twenty shiny, silver canoes lay across the rock-strewn sand, flipped over and resting upon one another. Rays of sunlight reflected from the aluminum hulls and temporarily blinded anyone who happened to glance that way. Scores of orange life preservers and black car tire inner tubes were stacked neatly behind the canoes, creating a colorful wall between the camp and the lake. Two platforms floated in the water about fifty feet from shore, bobbing up and down on the passing waves. Several empty 55-gallon steel barrels, secured to the underside of both wooden ten-foot square rafts, provided enough buoyancy to keep them afloat. The older kids pretty much hung out and played King of the

Mountain or some other roughhouse game on the rafts; the youngest campers squealed and splashed each other near the shoreline.

It was a picture-perfect, idyllic setting, excitement was at fever-pitch, and we all had a grand time during daytime hours. After dark, on the other hand, the nights became chilling and scary. Once dusk arrived, small campfires were lit in front of each cabin. The flickering orange and yellow flames grew in intensity, providing enough light for the twenty campers circling each of the 15 fire pits to see one another as they sat Indian-style on the hard ground. Every boy stared into the fire, seemingly hypnotized by the dancing flames, shadows, and light flickering across their excited faces. Every night during those two weeks, campers brought long, thin tree branches for toasting marshmallows; their faces filled with anticipation as the bag of spongy white treats made its way around the circle. Once the goodies were devoured, story time began!

The camp counselors (college students) must have taken a class to learn how to fuck with kids during camp. They usually told stories about werewolves, evil elves, deformed witches and deranged killers, who all resided within the deep ravines running along the two sides of our camp. These evil creatures were said to be extremely smart and knew to hide during the day. At night, they prowled the earth looking for kids to enslave and eat. In fact, some counselors testified that they'd seen these monsters wandering the campgrounds in the dead of night, watching them from behind trees and bushes until the coast was clear. Afterward, these college kids - entrusted to watch over us - prepared for their nightly antics.

For many, it was our first indoctrination to terror — there were many sleepless nights to follow!

Campers were divided and housed by age. As that was my first year there, I shared my cabin with nineteen other eight-year-old boys. Our parents were a hundred miles away, and the camp counselor's residences were across camp near the dining hall, leaving us all alone on that side of the property. Even though counselors took turns checking cabins twice each night, we were basically on our own to fend for ourselves... future third graders against the monsters of the night. We would soon become a Band of Brothers.

Once lights went out on that first night, spooky sounds and howling erupted from the far side of the camp; it was nothing like Halloween night, but just as chilling to us first-time campers. Grunts, cackling laughter, and dragging feet moved about through the darkness, calling out to the campers. One of them even walked the length of our porch, growling, banging on the wall and pulling something heavy across the wood planks. (Note to self: "Check for damage and scratch marks in the morning.") Twenty pairs of large white ovals shone in the darkness of the cabin, as eyes darted left to right, up and down, and followed the path of scary noises outside.

Everyone remained perfectly still in their bunks, afraid to make the slightest noise that might alert the monsters of their whereabouts. We remained on high alert for another twenty minutes until the sounds outside began to fade and then finally ceased. Unsure of our safety, we remained statue-like for several more minutes before getting the courage to lie back down.

51

Whispers began in earnest, questions circulating through the small cabin. I remember "hell" and "damn" were the only cuss words of choice at the time. None of us had a clue about the happenings outside and didn't care to find out. Some of the kids turned on their side and pulled blankets over their head, confident of their invisibility and security within the wool cocoons. The rest of us lay on our backs - some trying to sleep and others deep in thought - contemplating our fate for the remainder of the night.

About an hour later, the worst thing that could possibly happen, happened: one of the kids needed to use the bathroom. Our cabin was the last in the row and farthest from the facilities, which were almost two hundred feet away. Under normal conditions, it wouldn't have been such a big deal, but at that moment, we were all acutely aware of the monsters out there.

"No way I'm going out there!" the blond-haired kid in the last bunk against the wall volunteered.

Me neither!" another voice echoed.

Soon every camper in the cabin was shaking his head negatively and sharing his personal concerns with those on nearby bunk beds, each thankful for his own empty bladder. They carried on for the next ten minutes before it was quiet again and the campers settled down.

After another half-hour, a squeaking sound alerted those inside that the front door was opening. The old brass hinges creaked loudly in response to the shifting weight of the wooden door as it opened inward at a slow, creepy rate. As the crack widened, illumination from the half-full moon spilled into the room, eventually filling the frame of the open doorway.   Eyes peeked out from under blankets, their owners uncertain and fearful about what might happen next.

Suddenly, the silhouette of a small, pajama-clad boy appeared as he stepped into the doorway.   He didn't move from that spot, but his head turned slowly from side to side scanning the grounds to his front.

"Ralph, is that you?" someone called from within the cabin.

The silhouette turned to face the campers, "Yeah, Jerome, it's me."

"What are you doing?" his friend asked.   Others sat up again in their bunks, curious to see what was going on and thankful that a monster wasn't standing in the doorway.

"Jerome, I really gotta go," Ralph announced, his legs crossed, and his hands holding his crotch.   "Look, everyone! I don't see one monster running around outside, and it's quiet," Ralph stepped to the side and pointed out the doorway, "but I'm afraid to go by myself. Doesn't anybody else have to go?"

"Yeah, I do now," a small black in the third bunk commented, then pushed himself off the top mattress, landing gracefully as a cat.   He stood there briefly scratching his short black curly head and looked around the cabin, "Who else is comin' wif us?"

Ralph broke into a broad smile.

Jerome, Ralph's redheaded friend, got out of bed, "I'll come. Didn't have to go earlier but I have to now. What's your name?" he asked, facing the black kid.

" My name's Leroy, but everybody back home calls me 'Junior'."

*"Okay, "Junior" it is! Anybody else want to go?"
Ralph asked.*

*"Yeah, I'll come," I said, joining the other three kids at
the door. "My name is John. Seems like now I got to pee,
too. Besides, now that we're going in a group, it should be
safer if there's anything out there."*

*"Count me in," a chubby blonde kid announced. "I'm
Michael." He moved forward and joined the others.*

*The five of us gathered at the doorway, garbed in
various versions of sleeping attire: underwear, old T-shirts,
shorts, and the one boy lucky enough to own pajamas. Robes
were non-existent in our world. Nobody wanted to be the
first to step onto the porch into the cool night air. Clowning
around, we created a momentary logjam, mimicking the
Three Stooges before finally falling out on the porch
together and taking in the scene.*

*What looked – to us – to be a mile away, a single bulb
was visible over the facility door, casting a lemon yellow
aura as our beacon and guiding light through the pitch
black night.*

*It would be okay once inside; all we'd have to do was
twist the knob of the single wall switch to bathe the interior
in a light so bright it would feel like it was the middle of the
afternoon again. Running through the blackness barefoot or
in slippers was not advisable as the sharp stones, loose
branches and roots protruding from the ground could cause
some real boo-boos. We would need to tread carefully.*

*"What if one of those things the counselor told us about
is waiting for us out there?" Ralph asked.*

*"Yeah, them bad boys have night vision and can see in
the dark, you know!" Junior added.*

"Then we're toast!" I lamented. The five of us exchanged worried glances.

"We don't have a choice, guys." Michael pleaded, pointing to the side of the building. He continued, "I'm not peeing on the side of the cabin either."

Attempting to sneak a leak on the side of the cabin was risky because of the extreme darkness. A camper had to move slowly, inching through the damp weeds, arms extended and flailing about to identify any obstacles to his front, much like a blind person might do in unfamiliar surroundings. Spider webs hung everywhere; these arachnids especially liked to build their webs in the spacing between the horizontal logs of the cabin wall. Their sticky homes were as thick as a wad of cotton, and we all knew what resided therein, so using the wall as a guide was out of the question. Mosquitoes were also plentiful, thereby limiting the amount of one's pee-pee exposure time. The boys would have to wait until the absolute last moment before unbuttoning, as bites in that area would be bothersome for the rest of the night.

"Okay? On 'three'," I said. The five of us lined up at the edge of the porch like runners at the starting gates. "...One...Two...Three," we leaped to our fate. Unfortunately, for those scared little kids, venturing out into the night proved to be worse than imagined. As mentioned, those college kids loved to create havoc under the cover of darkness.

Picture five eight-year-old boys walking at a fast pace, wide-eyed and extremely anxious, on their trek through the dark open area en route to the bathroom. Unfortunately, they didn't notice one of the counselors lying in wait in a shallow depression, half-way to their destination. At just the right moment, he reached out and grabbed Ralph by the ankle, holding him tight and growling under his breath like a werewolf. Ralph screamed, crying out that something had grabbed his leg and wouldn't let go. Who came to his aid? No one! The rest of us took off running without looking back. When hearing Ralph's first shriek, the four of us elevated straight into the air like spooked kittens. We screamed in octaves higher than we believed possible. The four of us ran in place, banging into each other, until our little sneakers gained a foothold on the ground and launched us forward.

Several seconds passed before the counselor released his prey (Ralph) and crept away into the darkness. The poor kid hopped around like he was walking on burning coals, trying desperately to stay airborne and avoid whatever else might be on the ground. Suddenly alone, he panicked. His brain repeated instructions: 'run, run, run, get away!', but his body did not get the signals. Ralph, on the brink of crying now, took a deep breath and tried to pursue the others toward perceived safety. Much to his dismay, he had wet his pants and expressed his embarrassment after reaching the facility, standing breathless in front of his peers. Surprisingly, nobody laughed or made snide remarks about his encounter with one of those "things" or about wetting himself. The five of us stood huddled in a corner opposite the door, breathing heavily and seemingly in shock. Michael had tears streaming down his cheeks; he wasn't whimpering, but he stared silently out through the screened walls, oblivious to the others. My body quivered and my teeth chattered as if the temperature were below freezing.

Jerome quietly called for his mother, "Mommy, mommy, help me," sitting in a puddle of water by the showers, unfazed by his wet behind. Junior hopped up and down in front of the urinal, careful to keep his stream on target, hopeful that the movement would help empty his bladder faster.

It took almost an hour to compose ourselves and get cleaned up. During that time, we learned more about each other and formed a bond, promising one another that we would never run away again and leave one of us behind. Later in life, that would prove to be a difficult promise to keep to our buddies and fellow-soldiers; yet honor would compel us to do so.

We agreed on a plan and armed ourselves with mop handles, broomsticks, a dustpan and a toilet plunger from the supply closet. Imagining we were ready for anything and could now defend ourselves, the five of us locked arms and walked together in a horizontal line directly in front of the cabins until reaching our fortress. We hid the armaments under mattresses and atop the ceiling joists, confident that we now had weapons and could fight back. Our bravado lasted only another day before giving into fear again.

Often, these college guys donned masks and hid on the side of cabins, waiting for any kids that tried to sneak a leak there.

On one occasion, a camper had waited too long to pee, because nobody else needed or cared to run the distance to the bathroom with him, and he didn't want to risk going alone. Although relieving oneself on the side of the cabin was forbidden by the staff, this little guy knew he wouldn't make it to the bathroom in time and didn't have much choice. His body cramped from a full bladder, he walked stiffly, thinking it might burst. He had to pee right now! He slithered through the front door and moved slowly and cautiously to the side of the square structure, eyes wide open, but unseeing. Soon his extended arms came into contact with something unyielding. It wasn't a tree or bush but it felt hairy, rubbery and warm. The youngster inched forward, feeling around in hopes of identifying what stood in his way. He sensed movement and then heard a guttural moan emanating from the object. Suddenly, a beam of light flashed across the mask, momentarily revealing the face of an old man with long bushy eyebrows. He had shoulder-length gray hair, raw scars across his face and something looking like a bloody t-shirt hanging from his mouth. The little guy's scream woke all those campers inside, alerting them that one of their own was in trouble. However, none dared to get out of bed to help. Some pulled their blankets over their heads, cowering in fear, trying desperately to burrow deeper into their mattresses.

After a tense couple of minutes, the door suddenly banged open, startling those inside. The terrified youth fell through the doorway and onto the floor, his pajama shorts soaking wet, a puddle forming beneath him as he sat bewildered and breathing hard on the smooth plywood floor. His fellow eight-year-olds peeked out from their blankets, eyes wide as saucers, focusing on their cabin mate before them. In one swift move, he jumped to his feet, slammed the door closed and ran to his bunk, leaving a trail of urine in his wake. Ten minutes later, a camp counselor nonchalantly peeked in through the front door and asked if everything was okay. Not one of the kids dared to look toward the entrance for fear of seeing a creature in disguise, and nobody uttered a word in the darkness to give away their position.

Sneaking into the ravines bordering the camp in the dead of night was yet another havoc-wreaking ploy used by the counselors to scare us shitless. They would scream, howl, moan, and call out to the campers through the darkness, all the while making loud crashing sounds as they chased one another through the woods. Flashlight beams glowed through the night and on occasion, a red strobe light flashed in the distance, accompanied by the sound of a police car siren. Firecrackers popped to simulate gunfire against unknown creatures.

Some of the older kids snuck into the woods and ravines during the day but dared only to go so far before retreating to the safety of the open area. They reported seeing bodies hung from tree branches, blood splashed on trees, barbed wire with bits and pieces of clothing hanging from the barbs, and a sinister-looking cave on one end of the ravine. One of the explorers uncovered a worn, blue baseball cap from behind a bush with a dirty yellow camp emblem on the front. Another in the same group showed his findings: a yellow Pez dispenser and braided lanyard with an attached whistle, both of which had obviously been there for some time. The discoverer also pointed out that the mouth of the whistle appeared to have bite marks, as if a large feral animal had chewed on it. Traces of blood also remained on both the lanyard and whistle – both found not far from the dark cave entrance. Of course, all of this was food for thought and future nightmares!

The primary purpose of the camp was to provide us inner city kids with a couple of weeks of fun while we communed with nature. Little did we know that it also built character, taught us values, and gave us the opportunity to form friendships for years to come.

It took me another four summers before I began to get wise to the counselors. However, like good illusionists, those mischievous young staffers were slick at the stunts they performed, always leaving some room for doubt, and never letting us kids completely solve the camp's mysteries. One thing for certain, I learned the value of being a fast runner!

FIVE - LISTENING POST (2100 HOURS)

After Polack broke squelch once on the radio in response to the CP's request for a "sit-rep", he leaned over to poke LG's shoulder a couple of times with the handset to awaken him. LG nodded and silently unwrapped himself from his poncho liner cocoon. He slowly scooted up to a sitting position, ultimately leaning against the tree behind him. It was so dark that Polack could barely make out LG's profile. His boony hat was still pulled tightly over his head, its brim bent and wavy from lying on it. Anywhere else, Polack would have laughed out loud.

LG rolled his head and neck around his shoulders and shrugged to work out the kinks. Polack held out the radio handset, which LG accepted, and then placed it against his ear for the next two-hour shift.

Polack relished the idea of getting a couple hours of sleep and wrapped himself in his poncho liner, replicating LG's rest technique. Once lying down, however, Polack was far from comfortable. Because they arrived late at the position, neither of them had an opportunity to clean out a suitable sleeping spot. Branches, roots, and stones covered the ground and continuously poked their bodies, making for a tortuous night. In the morning, scrapes and bruises were visible reminders of their painful experience. Fortunately, over time, most soldiers became accustomed to sleep anywhere, anytime and under any conditions. To prove that point, Polack was already sound asleep and not the least bit aware of his discomfort.

LG soon felt an eerie sensation while sitting there, unable to see in any direction. Relentless mosquitoes flew Kamikaze missions, seeking out those uncovered areas on his face, neck, and hands. He didn't want to risk using more bug juice, because the pungent smell would be a sure indicator of their presence. Instead, he slowly lifted his poncho liner, blanketing himself as much as possible, leaving only a small opening for his eyes.

The sounds of the jungle continued to serenade LG, trying to lull him into Never Never Land. It was a struggle for anyone to stay awake in this kind of environment. LG continued to fight it, fully aware that falling asleep might get them - or others - at the firebase killed.

All at once, a distinct popping sound was heard and a small light became visible, pulsating at ground level some four-hundred meters behind them. Polack woke immediately and sat upright, joining LG, who was already fully focused in that direction. The light wasn't bright enough to lighten their immediate area, but the glow looked like the headlights of a far away locomotive.

Suddenly, the sound of an explosion near the light's source made them jump. Not loud enough to be a claymore mine or mortar round explosion, a grenade was the most likely culprit.

Polack looked at LG and pointed to the radio handset. LG shook his head negatively indicating that he hadn't heard anything over the radio about the incident.

After a long pause, they heard a deep thumping from the direction of the firebase, followed by a faint report in the sky. A brighter light appeared, unlocking the darkness below, exposing anything on the open ground between the firebase perimeter and the jungle. The overhead light, with its 500,000 candlepower, hung from a parachute and bobbed in the breeze. As updrafts and air currents manipulated the canopy, the artificial light rays hit the ground and shifted with every movement.

Both men immediately partially covered their eyes, shielding them from the glare to maintain their night vision. It was as if they had stared at a glowing light bulb for thirty seconds and then turned off the light – they could not see anything except the aftermath white glowing orb in the center of their vision. Had they not protected their eyes, Polack and LG's temporary blindness may have caused them to miss something important nearby.

The intense brightness of the overhead magnesium flare was still too far away to reveal the two men in their hiding place. Nevertheless, they remained perfectly still. Rays of light penetrated the jungle canopy and flickered across the vegetation. This also meant a company of enemy soldiers could either be heading in their direction or hiding in the dancing shadows, depending upon the viewer's mental state and level of imagination at the time. The floating candle burned for over a minute, continuously shedding a flickering light as it descended, its circle shrinking as it reached earth.

Both men drew the same conclusion about the earlier light and sound show. A trip flare must have ignited outside the perimeter, and one of the bunker guards reacted by tossing out a grenade near the burning light. The mortar crew then shot illumination rounds into the air to give the bunker guards enough light to do a visual recon of the area.

Satisfied that no enemy soldiers existed in the wire to their front, the nearby bunkers signaled "all clear" and the firebase returned to normal.

Sometimes rodents, small game, and even water buffaloes snagged the tripwires and ignited the flares. The early warning devices were set up within and to the front of the barbed wire surrounding the camp's perimeter. The nearest bunker opened fire if they spotted an enemy soldier in the flare light. Its occupants fired every weapon, blowing a claymore or two and throwing grenades out to their front. It was a formidable response.

Polack stayed awake with LG a bit longer, both of them listening for foot traffic creeping through the jungle between their position and the firebase. Enemy soldiers had a knack for appearing and then disappearing into thin air. If the enemy had indeed tripped the flare, it's likely that they'd hear him moving around to probe elsewhere on the perimeter.

LG responded to the 2200 hours request for a sit-rep with a single click on the handset. Polack sighed, hoping that he could get another hour of sleep before his next shift, and laid back down on his uncomfortable bed of brush.

Again, Polack was out within minutes. He fell into a deep state of sleep, dreaming about another childhood night of terror.

SIX - THE CEMETERY

My buddy, Paul, had a girlfriend who lived on a street adjacent to Mt. Olivet Cemetery, and when he visited her, I'd sometimes accompany him. As her house was a few miles away, it always took us about forty minutes to get there on our bicycles.

Once we arrived, Gloria from next door and a few of the other neighborhood kids walked over to join us on her porch. We'd sit on the steps of her small house, which directly faced the cemetery across the street, and often talked about all manner of weird stuff. Once, somebody mentioned a grave stone deep within the cemetery that spewed blood continuously every evening until midnight.

The neighborhood kids all remembered hearing about it but never chose to investigate. They were sure that something evil lurked there and had all warned each other to stay away. Paul and I heard of this bleeding gravestone before, and thought it might be an illusion of some sort, but one that we thought was worth checking out. The group shared our enthusiasm and supported the idea of breaking into the cemetery at night.

Mt. Olivet cemetery, built in 1888, is the largest cemetery in Detroit. Located on the east side of the city, it stands on over 300 acres of grass, gardens, and mostly maple and oak trees. The hulking, 19th century monuments that loomed over the plots are dark and Victorian, their presence at times spooky and intimidating, even during the day.

The main entrance was located on Van Dyke Avenue and Six Mile Road; the grounds spanned outward from that point and ran parallel to Van Dyke on the west and alongside Six Mile to the south. The North border ran alongside a diagonal set of railroad tracks crossing Van Dyke. Paul's girlfriend lived on Beland, a residential street that also happened to serve as the cemetery's eastern boundary.

Van Dyke and Six Mile were busy arteries in those days. Both streets hosted diners, factories, retail shops, a new car dealership, a bowling alley, and the northern boundary of the city airport. However, after dark, when the establishments closed for the day, the streets were empty, poorly lit, and still. A creepy aura spread beyond the cemetery fences, spilling onto the streets. Pedestrians avoided walking on the sidewalks next to the cemetery fence, and instead crossed over to the opposite side of the road. Nobody wanted to be near the property after dark and within reach of any ghosts or demons that might attempt to possess them.

Discussing the bleeding headstone for a couple of weeks, we finally agreed that a group would break into the cemetery and investigate this urban legend. In mid-July, darkness didn't set in until ten o'clock, so we only had a couple of hours to work with and locate this notorious landmark.

We resolved to carry out our plan on the following Wednesday, which was only two days away. The weatherman predicted a clear night and full moon; perfect conditions for us to sneak through the graveyard.

Paul and I arrived on our bikes at the rendezvous point a little after 9:30 p.m. and found several of our friends waiting in the shadows along the fence line. Eight of us had planned to go on this reconnaissance mission, but all four girls backed out. They claimed that boys were better suited to climb over fences, fight ghouls, and handle anything else that we might encounter. Ghouls! Hell, I never considered coming across evil spirits once inside. Now I was beginning to have second thoughts. The girls clearly used the female card to stay behind and had no intention of admitting they were just plain scared shitless. The guys, on the other hand, had an image to uphold and didn't want to appear to be sissies in front of the girls. As a consolation, at least we would not have to put on a show of bravado with the girls not there, and we could just be ourselves doing the deed.

It was time to go. Gloria and her friends offered words of encouragement and well wishes, promising to stay right there until we returned.

It was George, Jimmy, Paul and myself on this mission. Looking up at the towering fence before us, we could see that scaling it would clearly be the most challenging part of this adventure – at least we hoped that would be the worst part. The heavy wrought iron fence - designed to keep intruders out - stood menacingly before us. Each black three-quarter inch square steel baluster had a six-inch long spear-shaped ornament top; its overall height just a foot shy of a regulation basketball rim. Visions of impalement flashed through our brains, giving us pause and second thoughts of aborting the recon. However, boys being boys we would have done anything to look macho in front of females, even if it meant doing something exceptionally stupid that might get us critically injured.

Upper and lower three-inch wide rails ran horizontally along the expanse of the fence, two feet from both the top and bottom, providing stability and strength to the structure. It was designed to make it almost impossible to climb.

After fifteen minutes of brainstorming - as if we fourteen-year-olds were capable of doing so - Gloria returned, carrying two folded wool blankets in her arms. Standing on the bottom rail, I was able to drape both of them over the top of the balusters, thereby giving us a cushion and some protection against the sharp tips. I volunteered to be the first over.

As George was the largest and tallest of the group, we used him as a ladder to reach the upper rail. Jimmy and Paul helped me onto George's shoulders and then positioned themselves to catch me in case I fell. From there, I stepped onto the top rail, threw myself over to the other side, and slid down the baluster like a firefighter on a pole. This accomplishment resulted in subdued cheers and clapping from those on the other side. It only took a few minutes before the other three joined me.

It was time to set off and find the mysterious gravestone. The four of us walked side-by-side toward the interior; it reminded me of the scene in the "Wizard of Oz" where Dorothy and her companions walked through the deadly forest – but here there was no yellow brick road to follow, and no beacon to guide us through the darkness ahead.

We proceeded into the cool night air cautiously, keeping within an arm's reach of the guy next to us, holding onto his shoulder as we crept along. The tall trees soon blocked the rising moon from shining through the canopy, and each step was more precarious than the last. The old, ornate memorial statues would suddenly materialize in the darkness to give us a start. Angels poised in the air with shields and spears caused us to duck more than once. Still, no sign of the bleeding stone.

Hearing, but not seeing, the occasional vehicle passing on Six Mile Road, we changed direction and began shuffling that way. Suddenly Paul let out a muffled yelp and disappeared. We couldn't make out a thing around us and called out to him, groping about with our arms. The three of us started to panic and were about ready to take flight when we heard him cussing from the ground behind us. "Shit! Shit! Shit!". We found him sprawled out, and helped him to his feet. Apparently, Paul stepped onto a grave marker that had sunk into the ground. The sudden downward step caused him to lose his balance and fall to the ground. He thought he might have sprained his ankle, and he continued to spit out dirt and grass in between words. His open mouth had crashed into the damp earth as his face hit the ground.

I thought back to that first summer at camp when one of the boys in our group was grabbed by a mischievous counselor in the middle of the night while on his way to the bathroom. He screamed bloody murder, and the rest of us took off in a flash, scared beyond belief and leaving him alone to fend for himself. Luckily, Paul never found out how close I was to repeating history.

We only had another half-hour left before the apparition was said to disappear. We walked out from the copse of trees that had surrounded us and found ourselves stepping into the light of the now risen full moon. The ability to see changed our mood somewhat, but didn't help to eliminate the eeriness of the graveyard. We walked among the dead, intruding on hallowed ground, our fear of the unknown growing with every second.

Just then, George spotted a single vertical gravestone in the near distance and wordlessly pointed it out to us. A strange red pulsing glow emanated from it; a single entity standing alone, not sharing the warmth with its neighbors. Dropping to our knees, we continued watching in silence, hoping for some sort of sign that would unlock the baffling mystery before us.

None of us dared to venture any closer, afraid that some alien or paranormal force might be residing there. Paranoia took over. We continuously looked around, especially behind us, to ensure that nothing was sneaking up on us. We kept watching, but the stone's appearance remained unchanged. Was it bleeding? Was there a puddle of blood at the base of the stone? Imaginations began to soar and told us that it was far worse than anything we imagined. We pleaded with each other to agree to leave.

Suddenly, the headstone stopped bleeding! The four of us looked at one another in amazement. John looked at his glow-in-the-dark watch – a token from his Boy Scout days. Sure enough, it was midnight! Was it safe for us to go and check out the grave now? Nobody wanted to find out. Nobody cared. It was time to head back to the others. As we turned to make our way back, not one of the group notice that when the gravestone stopped "bleeding", it was at the exact moment that Klee's Bowling Alley on Six Mile Road had also turned off its red neon lights for the night. What was the chance that a reflection shone on only one single headstone sitting almost an eighth of a mile away? Needless to say, none of the masterminds in our group made that connection...

Hyped up and anxious to get back to our friends, we retraced our steps, still debating the details of the mystery. We were halfway through the dark stand of trees when a bright beam of light suddenly pointed directly at us. We froze, our feet rooted to the ground. A deep, guttural voice called out, summoning us to come to him. Not venturing to even sneak a peek behind us, we almost tripped over each other, attempting to get away. Running as if our lives depended on it, we continued in the direction of the fence line and our waiting friends. A bobbing beam of light behind us indicated that whatever it was, was still chasing us. Our minds were only able to focus on one thing - escaping this evil place.

Once we were close enough, we screamed out to our friends, warning them to run. They took off without question or a moment's hesitation. No teamwork existed this time when it came to scaling the fence. Every "man" for themselves. Pure fear drove us, and surges of adrenaline helped us to leap onto the upper rail and cross over without any help.

George was the first to get over, and once his feet hit the ground, he launched himself after the girls. I was next, and Jimmy followed a second or two later, both of us running after the retreating group. Paul was last to mount the fence and took a moment to dislodge the blankets from atop the spears, tossing them to the ground. Unbeknownst to him, one of the top fence spears snagged his pant leg as he leaped over, causing his body to slam into the other side of

71

the fence. Paul hung precariously for a second before the spear ripped through his pants, tearing the material from his thigh to the ankle. He fell to the ground in a heap, knocking the wind out of himself for the second time in less than an hour. Not seeing any evidence of the pursuer or his beam of light, Paul laid there panting, taking a moment to catch his breath.

Meanwhile, the seven of us huddled on Gloria's porch; George, Jimmy, and I - extremely animated in our descriptions – relayed all that we saw or imagined. The girls watched us, eyes wide, mouths agape, listening intently and thankful they didn't go with us. We wondered aloud about Paul, hoping that he didn't get caught - or something worse. Sure, we were worried about him, but none of us could summon the courage to go back to look for him.

A slow moving shadow on the street caught our eye. We all held our breath and watched without speaking. Suddenly, the shadow walked into the glow of an overhead street light two houses down. A second later, Paul materialized out of the dark. He was disheveled, bent over, limping badly, the full length of his left ripped pant leg was blotched with blood, and he wasn't smiling. None of us laughed. We sat perfectly still, most of us wondering if a ghoul had captured him, or if he had somehow become possessed. Paul shuffled toward the porch and tossed both blankets to Gloria. Not knowing what to expect, we remained poised and ready to run if Paul snarled at us. He finally spoke and said sharply, "Thanks for all your help back there. You guys left me to the wolves!"

None of us could respond. 'Shit, he's a werewolf now!' I thought, inching my way off the cement slab.

"Are you okay?" his girlfriend asked.

Paul finally dropped onto the ground, drawing his knees up and wrapping them with both arms. "I'll be okay. Just a bit of bad luck."

We gathered around, hanging on to every word, listening to Paul intently as his woeful tale unfolded. Grateful that he wasn't caught, bitten, or possessed, we began to relax in his presence. Although we all felt really bad about what had happened to him - and felt guilty about leaving him in the lurch - we couldn't help but feel relieved that we had survived our night of terror.

It was fear that made our self-preservation instincts kick in; once again, running was our first – and best – response to that fear.

SEVEN - LISTENING POST (2200 HOURS)

Polack's eyes suddenly flashed open, unmoving, looking straight up, momentarily unsure of his whereabouts. The hand that suddenly clamped over his mouth had startled him and brought his brain back to the real world. His body stiffened, adrenaline now coursing through it, preparing to fight off this attacker and defend himself.

He felt something fuzzy rubbing against the left side of his face, then hot, rapid breathing in his ear before hearing a single whispered word: "Gooks." Polack recognized LG's voice and realized that the bristling sensation on his face was LG's Afro brushing against him. "Stay down and don't move," the whisper commanded. Polack turned his head slightly to face LG, their noses only an inch apart, then acknowledged that he understood with a single nod. Seeing this, LG slowly slid his left hand away from Polack's mouth and let it drop to his partner's chest. He felt his partner's chest rise and drop with every deep breath, the rapid heartbeat matching his own.

LG was sprawled along the ground, his head propped up against Polack's shoulder, the radio handset wedged tightly between Polack's left shoulder and LG's right ear.

It was 2245 hours when LG first heard the movement in the jungle on the other side of the trail they had used earlier. It started out with the sound of footsteps occasionally stepping on dried branches, loud crackling noises carrying through the night. As the group moved closer, LG heard machetes cutting through the thick vegetation, followed by harsh protests in Vietnamese. LG was confident that the group was heading directly toward their position. Right before waking Polack, LG had keyed the handset and whispered, "Lima Papa 1," then broke squelch twice in rapid succession to indicate they had detected movement.

A barely-audible voice responded to LG's raised alarm, "Roger, Lima Papa 1, be advised there are no friendlies near your poz. Thunder 3, standing by."

Polack and LG listened intently to the action coming from their right, both blind to the actual presence, only sure they were hearing an enemy force of unknown size. They tried to burrow deeper into the slight depression they were in, and fought every impulse to run back to the firebase.

Now, fully awake, Polack realized that all of the jungle sounds had ceased. In itself, this was a sure sign that invaders were moving within their realm. The birds and insects, like both men in the LP, stayed perfectly still, quiet and out of sight, waiting until the threat had subsided.

Instead of crossing over the trail and continuing their march toward LG and Polack, the point man turned east on the trail, the rest of the column numbly following in his footsteps. The two hidden men prepared to take a deep breath and exhale in relief, when to their horror, the column stopped to drop in place for a break. Less than twenty feet away, the two Americans gnashed their teeth and silently mouthed, 'Oh, shit!' They also discovered that they were still holding their breath, both reluctant to exhale in the event that the enemy would hear them. Any sound or movement at all would inevitably expose their hiding place.

The first order of business was to control their labored breathing and get a grip.

The enemy soldiers squatted on the trail and began talking among themselves in whispered tones. Several of them lit cigarettes; glowing ends flickered through the darkness like mosquito chasers the kids used back home. The scent of marijuana also permeated the air, another sign that this group was overly confident and unafraid of those in the firebase only 500 meters away.

Polack and LG were stunned at the blatant disregard for silence and stealth this close to the firebase. Both hoped that the bunker guards on the firebase didn't suspect something to their front and begin shooting or firing mortars in their direction. That would surely be the end of the LP.

While Polack and LG were pondering their immediate future, two enemy soldiers ventured away from the trail and into the brush on the LP's side of the path - one to their front and the other behind them. LG and Polack stiffened, both sucking in their breath again. The movement of the soldier to their front finally stopped about fifteen feet away. They both clearly heard him urinating, his stream forceful, steady, and splashing against the foliage. After what seemed like two full minutes, the spattering of liquid slowed and then finally stopped several seconds later. All at once, LG gripped Polack's arm in a panic and whispered slowly into his ear, "The Claymores."

'Fuck' was the only word coming to mind when they remembered the layout, then realized that the one closest to the trail was at the highest risk of discovery. Of course, in this darkness, it was impossible to see the mine or the wire leading away into the thick brush. Only stepping on it or

tripping over the wire would expose it. Polack was already holding the firing mechanism for that particular mine; the safety was off, and he prepared to squeeze the handle in the event that the enemy soldier discovered it. Blowing the mine would vaporize him and a portion of his comrades on the trail. Retaliation would be immediate; the surviving enemy soldiers would then spray lead in every direction. The odds of surviving such an onslaught would be nil.

Both waited and prayed that their luck would hold out while the enemy soldier moved back through the foliage toward his companions. They couldn't see him, but could hear his movements. He was extremely noisy, "probably wearing clown shoes", and extremely close. When no alarm sounded, both LP's almost whistled, exhaling the breath they'd been holding in.

'How long are they going to hang around? I hope they can't hear my heartbeat or hear my breathing...I am so fucking scared!'

The sound of the man moving behind them was just as alarming. He seemed to be moving as if he were searching for something. The enemy soldier continued until he was even with their position and then stopped just ten feet away from Polack and LG. Upon stopping, he kicked at the foliage and stomped on the ground a few times. A long drawn out note announced his passing of gas followed quickly by a deluge of diarrhea that hit the earth in a splat. He was loud, and grunted continually. The smell was worse than the stench of a week-old, dead, bloated body. His fellow soldiers must have been chiding him about the noise and odor; several called out in urgent sing-song tones. He responded right away with a snide remark of his own; it must have been funny because those nearby guffawed. A sharp command from further up the trail interrupted the laughter and quickly silenced the group.

The LP's had been enjoying the light breeze blowing steadily from the west; it triggered cold chills when passing over their sweat- drenched bodies and was a blessed relief from the tropical heat. Now, however, now they both cursed that wind. The smell of his waste wafted through their position; the two men pinched their noses closed so they wouldn't retch. Once finished with his business, the soldier pulled up his trousers and returned to his group without covering his excrement, thus leaving the Americans a gift to cherish for the rest of the night.

At 2315 hours, the sound of snapping fingers and a gruff command caused a commotion out on the trail. The enemy soldiers stopped their chattering, gathered up their gear and within a minute, set out in an easterly direction along the hard-packed path, right toward Rock's ambush position some distance away.

'Oh my God...oh my God...they're finally gone!'

"We got to let Rock know they're comin' his way," LG whispered into Polack's ear. Polack placed his forefinger over his lips to silence his partner. They waited an extra ten minutes before risking movement, sitting up, or speaking.

The radio frequency had remained silent since LG first informed the CP of their situation almost a half-hour earlier. True to protocol, Thunder 3 had postponed the hourly sit-reps, and everyone on that channel stood by, anxious for an update.

"How many do you think were out there?" LG asked in a barely audible whisper.

Polack bent close to LG's ear, "I'd guess at least twenty."

"Yeah, I'm hip to that. Did you see anything?"

"Come on, G, did YOU?"

"Well, I had to ask."

"I do think they might be carrying something heavy because when they stopped, I heard a couple of them grunt and drop something big to the ground."

"You thinking mortars?"

"Yeah, big ones, G!"

"I'd bet they broke bush just inside the jungle and were scoping out the south side of the firebase."

"If that's what you think, better pass that info on to the CP. I wasn't awake until just before they broke out onto the trail."

"Okay, that's what I'll call in."

"You want me to do it so you can crash for a while? I was supposed to start my watch a half hour ago."

"Are you fuckin' crazy?" LG sputtered. "There is no fuckin' way I'm gonna lay back down until the jungle creatures start singin' again."

"I hear ya'," Polack agreed. "Call it in and I'll keep listening for them to return."

LG covered himself with his poncho liner and lay on the ground. Whispering continued back and forth for the next fifteen minutes as LG filled in the CP with all of their theories. Polack heard absolutely nothing of the conversation taking place, which pleased him. When LG finished with his report to the CP, he requested permission for both of them to return to the firebase since such a large group of enemy soldiers was in the area. Permission was denied.

At the midnight hour, Thunder 3 began a new round of sit-rep requests. Polack keyed the handset once in response; back to business as usual.

Almost two clicks east of the LP's position, Rock prepared his squad for the possibility of fighting a force twice as large as theirs. The location of their ambush site was a good choice and well-suited for taking on a much bigger force. Mechanicals (trip-wire activated Claymore mines) covered both avenues of approach on the same trail, and a third, set up across the road on a small pathway, would catch any enemy soldiers retreating in that direction. Large fallen tree trunks ran across the length of their ambush site affording each squad member some protection. The squad also beefed up their defenses by setting up manually activated mines between themselves and the road. The anxious men remained on one hundred percent alert.

Back at the LP, the jungle sounds soon revved up and were almost back to normal. With LG sound asleep, Polack soon felt safe enough to again revisit his past.

EIGHT - GHOST STORIES

I'll always remember those times when a group of us went to visit a fellow classmate, Carmen. Her mother often told us stories about spirits and people coming back to life; this was way before we'd ever heard of zombies. Unbeknownst to us at the time, her culture celebrated death and spirits, and her kin worshiped their ancestors. To us teens, we thought 'Mama Devilme' was a voodoo priestess or something, but dared not to ask or get on her bad side - none of us wanted her to curse us for life. To us, everything she told us was plausible and made sense! After all, who could make up stories like this?

Carmen's great-grandparents originally came from Haiti and settled in Louisiana; most of her relatives also lived there. When the families visited, much of their conversations revolved around Voodoo and messages from Baron Samedi or other spirit Barons who ruled the dead. Years later, the 1973 James Bond movie "Live and Let Die" popularized a villain who took on the role of this Baron to scare the locals. That culture held the Barons in high regard, and evenings on Carmen's porch were our first introduction to Haitian mythology.

We'd all get together at Carmen's house at least weekly during the summer months before our junior year in high school, listening intently to her mom's tales. The sun had set and the heat of the day had dissipated. Sometimes a breeze washed over the group, giving us a chill that sent goosebumps up and down our arms and legs or made neck hairs stand on end. She spoke slowly, in almost a whispering tone; the attention to detail created clear pictures in our heads, making it easy for us to follow along. Carmen's mother spoke reverently of the spirits and sometimes warned us of things not to do. She appeared fearless and sometimes seemed to lapse into a trance. We were in awe, but felt safe and protected in her presence.

For the life of me, I can't recall any of the stories Mama Devilme told, but I remember being on high alert while walking home. Her tales continued to play out in our heads; both the quiet darkness and fear forced our imaginations into overdrive. Every parked car, tree, and bush served as possible hiding places for demons, spirits and ghosts, so we made a point of scrutinizing them when passing.

The girls in our group lived nearby and split away from us guys within the first two blocks. We then had to cross over the expressway bridge and walk an additional several blocks to get to our homes.

It was usually close to midnight when we left Carmen's house, and since storytime normally occurred on a weekday, the streets were mostly bare, silent and dark. Only a few porch lights provided a hint of illumination, overtaking the shadows on the sidewalk. The street lights directed a sphere of light downward onto the pavement, providing a brief respite from the dark.

During our walk home, we'd all be deep in thought about Mama Devilme's stories. Initially, there 'd be some light chatter when the girls were still with us, but now - fifteen minutes later - one only heard sneakers shuffling on the sidewalk.

I can't explain it, but this happened every time: one person in our group would think they heard something ominous or saw something hiding in the nearby bushes and would suddenly sprint away. Those remaining had absolutely no idea of what spooked our friend, but within a single heartbeat, we were all following and running for our lives with heads turned every which way, looking for the threat. We'd all run fast and hard, with nobody saying a word. Finally, we'd stop at the end of the block to catch our breath. Each of us gasped for air, bent over with hands on our kneecaps to keep us from collapsing. As we tried to slow our rapid breathing, our heads would turn, looking deep within the shadows behind us for an answer. Once it came, we never questioned each other. If one person thought he heard or saw something alarming, that was good enough for the rest of us. Later - once we felt secure and were thankful that we were still whole - we all laughed about the incident and then poked fun at each other, mimicking the contorted faces of terror we made during the run for our lives. After we calmed down, the trek home continued without further incident.

We followed the same route home every week; guys peeled off as they reached their homes and the rest of us continued onward. It was funny watching them quickly scamper up the stairs and exhibit an exaggerated sigh of relief when reaching the porch.

As it turned out, Wayne and I were always the last two remaining because we lived the farthest away. As close friends in the neighborhood, we made a pact some time ago and agreed to split the difference, so I wouldn't have to walk so far by myself. We passed Wayne's house, continuing together for another block to the halfway point between our houses. On a silent signal and nod, we'd split up and run in two different directions to reach home, not stopping until we were inside the front door.

I may have scared my mother on occasion when I barged through the front door, bent over and breathing hard. She'd jump up from her chair with a confused look on her face. "What's wrong?" she'd ask, the expression slowly changing to one of worry. She'd push past me, then lift the side of the shade and peek out. "Who's chasing you?"

"Nobody, Mom!" I replied between gasps. "I just left Wayne and wanted to get home quickly." She frequently didn't believe me and would continue to look out the window, searching the street for several more seconds.

"You kids are going to kill me," she scolded, then settled back into her chair, refocusing her attention on the television.

One of those times when I was racing home, I spotted my younger sister and some of her friends chatting on our front porch. I stopped suddenly and sidestepped into the shadows of our neighbors' lawn where they couldn't see me. Standing there in the darkness, I attempted to catch my breath and slow down the rapid beating of my heart. My pride wouldn't allow them to see me in my state of panic. When I got myself together, I stepped back onto the sidewalk and began walking like a great pimp in the night. None of the girls saw me approaching until I was on the walkway leading to the porch; the nearest girl yelped in fright, which visibly startled the others.

"Oh, it's only my brother," my sister dismissed. Relieved, the others started giggling.

"Where are you coming from?" she demanded. Four pairs of eyes pierced through the darkness awaiting my response. I recognized their faces from earlier visits to the house. My sister, Christine, was having another sleepover with her twelve year-old friends. All wore shortie pajamas and snuggled up together on the glider. A folding snack table in front of them held a large bowl of Better Made potato chips and four chilled glasses of Vernors "pop" - Detroit's nickname for soda.

"A bunch of us were at Carmen's listening to her mom tell stories," I told her nonchalantly.

"And you walked all the way from her house?" she gasped incredulously.

"Yeah, it's not far." I reached into the bowl of chips and grabbed a handful before turning to the door.

"Yes, it is!" Christine declared emphatically. Looking at her friends, she continued, "She lives way on the other side of the expressway, more than a mile away," she explained and pointed to the west. Christine turned back toward me. "It's late! Weren't you scared out there by yourself?" she asked.

I chuckled at the question. "Of what? The boogeyman?" I mused, as the girls looked at one another with saucer-sized eyes.

"Not funny! Somebody could have jumped you!" Christine scolded. "Guys from that street gang, the LaGrand Boys, have been driving up and down the street and have jumped whites for no reason at all. I heard it's part of their initiation into the gang or something! Just the other day, my friend's brother got beat with a baseball bat and got hurt real bad!"

"Yeah, I heard about him. He was a dumbass for walking through their territory. At least I know better to stay a couple of blocks this side of their street."

"I know you can't outrun a car!" Sis challenged.

"No, but I can jump fences and get away from a car. Remember, this is our neighborhood, and I know some pretty clever hiding places if I'm chased. Besides, if they tried to jump me, I can take care of myself," I bragged, puffing out my chest and opening the screen door.

"Don't say I didn't warn you," Christine called as I walked into the house. Through my peripheral vision, I could see the other girls becoming animated and begin talking all at once. I couldn't quite make out their conversation and only caught a word here and there: "...brave...wow...I couldn't..." Thankfully, my act was successful. Had I not seen them when I did, I would have surely been embarrassed by my fear and would never hear the end of it.

On the way to my bedroom, I thought about the gang comment Christine made and shuddered. Who was I fooling? It IS dangerous out on the streets. Along with the LaGrand Boys, street gangs like the Bishops and Chene Gang routinely sought out one another. The Harper Recreation Bowling Alley was only a couple blocks from my home; gang fights erupted periodically in the parking lot on Saturday nights. Handguns were rare at that time, so combatants fought with fists, bats, pipes, chains and knives; blood splotches were often visible on the pavement the following morning. Motorcycle gangs such as the Highwaymen and Renegades regularly scuffled in the parking lots of both the Top Hat and White Castle restaurants on Eight Mile and Gratiot Roads. These were older guys in their 20's, and once the fights started, an exodus of cars left quickly for fear of damage to their cars or person. Word on the street was that the Purple Gang was still active, but their members were much older and supported other causes.

In hindsight, looking back at my youth, running was always the immediate response to fear. I wondered at what age that would finally stop. My sister and her friends never did find out the truth about "Christine's brave big brother, John" ...that is, until now.

NINE - LISTENING POST (MIDNIGHT)

Jungle insects and other nocturnal creatures resumed playing their exotic music. The earlier infiltration of their habitat no longer posed a threat; it was safe again to seek out mates. Their activity and sound provided a calming effect on those humans nearby in the Listening Post.

Polack suddenly stiffened, turned his head slightly and tried to focus in the darkness. Listening intently, he waited for the specific sound to repeat itself. The symphony continued at full tilt; crickets and monkeys seemingly making the most noise. He heard the faint fluttering of a bird overhead as it flitted from tree to tree. Then, all at once, the bird called out in the darkness, "REEEE-UP...REEEE-UP...REEEE-UP". It sounded like the deep baritone croak of a frog – nothing like a bird. It moved to another location and repeated its mating call. There was no response, but nevertheless, Polack smiled broadly, glad to have the bird to keep him company.

One specimen of lizard in the jungle had an unusual mating call that sounded like a bathtub floating toy when squeezed. Its call was high-pitched and completed in two parts. The first, sounding like "FAAA" was sort of a whistle, a sharp trill that rose in octaves. The second sounded more like a sigh, "CUE", as if the lizard were exhaling. Together, its mating call sounded like "FAAA-CUE...FAAA-CUE."

On some occasions, these two creatures were both nearby and called out to one another. The bird called out, "REEE-UP" (an acronym for re-enlisting in the military) and the lizard responded with "FAAA-CUE." Sometimes it would go on for hours and it was hilarious.

Both the Blue Eared Barbet bird and Tokay Gecko Lizards are plentiful in the jungles of Vietnam; each call out to mates during the still of night, and would often keep American soldiers company during their nightly watches. Their croaks and whistles were well known to the men. However, both creatures were better known by their slang names: "re-up bird" and "fuck you" lizard. That night, both serenaded Polack.

A mortar flare suddenly popped overhead, close to the treeline and near the LP position, interrupting Polack's symphony. Hearing this noise, LG awoke instantly and joined Polack in watching the bright light nearby. It burst in the sky right where the treeline and the east trail intersected. An hour ago, it would have caught the enemy platoon by surprise while they took their break.

Every creature immediately stopped its chatter once the flare exploded, remaining still while the light pulsated over the area. The breeze continued to blow from the west and soon carried the parachute over the LP's position. Both men froze, knowing full well that movement in the flickering light is exaggerated and would be bound to expose them. The flare, like a spotlight, showered both men with throbbing beams of light. Their only choice was to keep still and continue watching their front, riveted until the light went out. Everything appeared surreal and shifted under the floating torch, opening the door to their imaginations. The parachute soon snagged on a treetop and burned itself out. Although the harrowing experience lasted just a few minutes, it felt like their lives had been suspended for an hour.

It was now 0045 hours. LG decided to stay awake since his watch was starting in another fifteen minutes anyway, and he urged Polack to take his break. However, something still wasn't right. Several minutes had passed since the spotlight went out, and the jungle creatures should have been singing again. The quiet concerned both men, who quickly returned to a guarded posture. They remained silent and still, both wishing they had super powers to help identify any threat. *'Why did the firebase fire the flare in the first place when nobody radioed in to ask for illumination? Did they see something? Were they looking for the enemy platoon?'* Both asked themselves the same questions and then paused as if some higher power was going to answer them. *'Why didn't the enemy column run into Rock's ambush by now? It was highly impossible that the enemy platoon passed undetected. They are still out there somewhere between the LP and Rock's position.'* Polack and LG's sense of foreboding moved up a few notches. They fidgeted some to get more comfortable and tried desperately to spot anything in the pitch black darkness.

Suddenly, they heard the sound of a mortar tube firing some distance away: "Thunk…Thunk…Thunk." Without knowing the target, both LP's buried themselves into the ground and prayed that the rounds weren't heading their way. Polack reached up and grabbed ahold of the good luck charm hanging from his neck, squeezed it tightly in the palm of his right hand, then said a silent prayer for his protection.

After what felt like an eternity, three back-to-back explosions sounded from within the firebase, "Crump – Crump – Crump." The blasts were loud and violent, sounding much larger than 60 mm rounds, and were most likely 82 mm mortar rounds. Polack and LG breathed a sigh of relief and then raised their heads skyward in thanks. Just then, the Red Alert alarm in the new firebase began wailing, and sounding like a fire engine siren in slow motion, the tempo became faster as the seconds passed. Several rounds of illumination launched from the firebase, popping high above the camp perimeter, focusing more on the eastern side. All at once, LG and Polack heard the enemy mortar fire again: "Thunk...Thunk... Thunk", from the same location meant three more rounds on the way. Seconds later, "Crump...Crump...Crump," announced the rounds impacting deeper into the firebase perimeter.

Polack had informed Thunder 3 right after the first three rounds were fired. He provided an azimuth from the LP and estimated the distance at 300 meters, possibly more. Rock had also heard the firing and forwarded the direction and distance from his position. Once the information was received and plotted, a single 105 mm round fired from the battery, erupting some distance to the front of the LP. Rock quickly made a correction: "add one-hundred, left one-hundred." The artillery group was still calculating the new trajectory when the enemy mortars let loose with another volley of three rounds. The cannon fired once more before the artillery crew took cover - the mortars landed just outside the battery's sandbagged enclosure. While the cannoneers recovered, Rock saw that the 105 mm shell landed right where he wanted, and called into the handset,

"On target, fire for effect!" Seconds later, the entire battery of six cannons fired in unison; the sound almost deafening to the men downrange as the large guns fired in their direction. The projectiles passed overhead and sounded like an express commuter train rushing past a platform. Their detonations reverberated across the ground and lifted the two men into the air after each volley. The battery fired four more times, sending a total of twenty-four high explosive rounds overhead. Small adjustments between volleys allowed the gunners to move the detonations around and saturate the general area. The enemy mortar crews were silenced after the first full-battery volley.

The LP could see flickering flames in the distance as small fires erupted in the vicinity of the detonations. There was plenty of dead wood laying about and the chance of them burning out quickly was not going to happen. From this distance, the dense vegetation made the glowing flames look more like a handful of flashlights or small camp fires. They were also glad that a giant forest fire wouldn't engulf them in a few hours - no need to be concerned about that due to the moist, verdant foliage. One less thing to worry about!

Thankfully, the brass opted not to send out a patrol into the area looking for bodies. The officers there were more concerned about the safety of their people instead of sending them out to count bodies and collect souvenirs. *'Moving through this pitch black jungle at night would be suicide...how can Charlie continuously do it? Oh, that's right... this is his backyard!'*

Thunder 3 informed everyone tuned into the frequency that the enemy mortar crew must have had a spotter with a radio somewhere near the camp perimeter, as the placement of the enemy rounds was just too accurate for chance hits.

'Fuck,,,fuck...fuck!' Hearing this new information, Polack and LG understood that changes would need to be made in their position. Earlier, it wasn't a big deal to keep tabs on the area behind them because it was assumed the firebase monitored it. Now that there was a possibility that someone might be sneaking around behind them, it was necessary to watch a full 360 degrees around their position.

Both men scooted around to the side of the trees they'd been using as backrests; one man now faced north and the other south. When looking east now, both men could see a lighter backdrop about 200 meters away, due to the small fires still smoldering here and there. They weren't bright enough to lighten the jungle, but would make it possible to spot a silhouette in that direction, in the event that the enemy was lurking nearby.

This was where the jungle ended and the bulldozed clearing began. Everything was still dark when looking over that way, but at least, trees, branches, and hanging vines were now able to be identified. Both men were now confident that if an enemy soldier with a radio dared to cross against the lighter backdrop, he'd be easily recognized.

'What do we do if we see him? Too far for a grenade, can't shoot at him from the LP, bunkers can't open fire without putting us in danger. We'll have to call it in and let the powers that be decide. They'll probably use mortars. Maybe a sniper. Maybe a gunship. Shit...Shit...Shit!'

About thirty minutes later, the jungle creatures began stirring again and celebrating, their calls excited and urgent this time. Even though the full symphony resumed a few moments later, Polack and LG still felt uneasy and remained on one hundred percent alert. The enemy spotter, mortar crew, and missing enemy platoon were still out there, all were intent to kill Americans under the cloak of darkness.

TEN - LISTENING POST (0100 HOURS)

LG had the radio handset to his ear when Thunder 3 called at 1 a.m. for the sit-rep that was scheduled every hour. The monotone voice sounded like the soldier on duty was both tired and burned out; he struggled through the calls, hesitating at times for several seconds before calling the next unit on the list. Those who listened guessed that he was either dozing off or bleeding off his adrenaline surge from the camp's earlier mortar barrage, and was now both physically and mentally exhausted.

The jungle serenade continued in earnest, leaving both men in the LP more comfortable and relaxed. Thirty minutes passed since Thunder 3's last check, and Polack seriously contemplated his option to go back to sleep, leaving LG to complete his watch alone.

Polack tapped LG's shoulder, ready to inform him that he was turning in, when suddenly a bright flash lit up the jungle to their southeast, immediately followed by a thunderous explosion, startling both of them. Gunfire erupted, sounding at first like a single M-16, then growing in intensity as others joined the fray. Seconds later, three smaller explosions sounded - possibly grenades - echoing in the darkness before the deep, throaty sound of an M60 machine gun began. The distinct pop-pop sound of AK-47s soon joined the cacophony of sound. Red and green tracer rounds ricocheted into the air, and went skipping across the sky like shooting stars.

It quickly dawned on Polack, LG, and everyone else in the firebase that Rock's team blew the ambush, most likely catching the roving NVA platoon in one of their Claymore booby traps out on the trail.

The two men in the LP sat mesmerized by the fireworks show before them. They would have remained that way had it not been for a couple of errant rounds that zipped past their position.

"Down!" barked Polack, grabbing LG and pushing his friend into a prone position. "Some of those rounds just missed us overhead!"

"I heard them, too." LG stammered. "We both shoulda' known better than to just sit here watching the firefight." LG curled up into a fetal position, hoping to make his body less of a target.

"You got that right, bro!" Polack agreed.

The firing intensified; the telltale sound of a fully engaged automatic firefight carried across the darkness. Just then, the sound of a second tremendous blast drowned out the rifle fire and once again, lit up that portion of the dark jungle.

'Another Claymore exploding,' Polack thought to himself.

Soldiers in the firebase reacted differently to the melee. The stand-by reactionary force had secured their supplies and were already moving toward the main gate. They'd wait there, ready to move out in support of the ambush team if they called for help. Those in bunkers stood on top and watched the exploding fireworks display; others came out of their hooches to do the same. Everyone hoped for the best and silently prayed for their brothers-in-arms.

LG and Polack were more vigilant now, listening intently, trying to block out the sounds of battle so they could hear approaching movement in their direction. The jungle inhabitants had stopped their mating calls and chattering immediately after the initial explosion, thus helping the two LP soldiers to better concentrate on their sector.

"Listen up, Polack! Some of them motherfuckers may be coming our way!"

"I'm on it, brother!" Polack affirmed.

Whenever the enemy force walked into an ambush, they'd usually try to circle and counter-attack the Americans from their flanks. If that strategy failed, they'd disperse and soon disappear, often taking their dead and wounded comrades with them to psyche out the Americans. Without bodies, the Americans were unable to determine the enemy size and casualties from the resulting firefight. Not finding anything - especially when the return fire was unyielding - the average GI felt disappointment and began to doubt his efforts. If he lost a fellow soldier and friend in the fight, then his thoughts and feelings were magnified tenfold, the guilt began to manifest itself, and depression would set in.

After what seemed like fifteen minutes, but was actually no longer than four minutes, Rock's agitated voice broke through the squelch on the radio channel, "Thunder 3, this is Alpha Romeo 6, over." Sounds of gunshots and mayhem from the firefight were heard in the background.

"This is Thunder 3, go ahead!" The battalion CP radio operator coaxed, much more lively now. By this time, most of the camp officers had also crowded into the small command bunker, awaiting word about the gunfight to their east.

"Roger, Thunder 3. Be advised that we've engaged an enemy force of unknown size. Requesting a fire mission on preset location Alpha-Alpha-Niner, over."

"Wilco, stand by," the radio operator responded.

The rate of fire had slowly subsided. Rock's group switched their weapons to semi-automatic to pick targets and shoot at flashes from the surrounding foliage. The pop-pop sounds of AK-47 fire continued, but were more sporadic now compared to their momentum earlier.

Thunder 3's voice returned on the frequency, "Shot out!" A single cannon fired from the firebase; the 105 mm round screamed overhead en route to the preset coordinates determined earlier at the firebase. A loud "CARUMPT!" announced its arrival; the single detonation sounded even louder than the two larger explosions heard minutes before.

"On the mark," Rock reported. "Fire for effect!"

"Roger, firing for effect," Thunder 3 echoed after a two-second delay.

Almost immediately, the six cannons let loose once again with the first barrage into that area. The high-explosive rounds impacted on target, and lit up the jungle in an awe-inspiring display of firepower. Several small fires ignited as red-hot shrapnel found the dead rotting wood throughout the impact area.

Polack and LG covered their ears; the impact shook the jungle and bounced both soldiers a few inches off the ground. The sharp smell of cordite and smoke soon reached the LP; a by-product of the sustained firefight usually accompanied by the smoky fog of expended gunpowder.

Even though the two LP's couldn't see through the darkness, both felt the thick fog entering their lungs.

Rock adjusted his fire after each barrage, moving the next rounds farther away and more in the presumed direction of the fleeing enemy. He called for a cease-fire after just three volleys.

Seconds later, multiple flares popped over the ambush area, basking the dark, eerie jungle below in a yellow flickering, smoke-filled aura.

The two men in the LP sat up straight, and nervously focused on their front. Instinct dictated that since the enemy platoon passed this way earlier, some of the survivors might return and stumble into their position.

While Lima Papa 1 pondered their future, members of Rock's ambush team stepped out of their location and began reconnoitering and securing the immediate area. Two of his men were injured, suffering from gunshots and shrapnel wounds; a Medivac chopper was on its way to pick them up and transport both to a hospital.

A small perimeter soon formed around the ambush site. Each soldier faced outward and watched for movement under the canopy of flickering light. Within minutes, the Dustoff chopper arrived, its escort of two gunships circled overhead like protective angels. As landing was impossible, both soldiers had to be lifted up through the dense foliage on a jungle penetrator - a cable and seat contraption used to extract injured soldiers in situations just like this. Two minutes later, both wounded men were safely aboard the unarmed Huey. The helicopter dipped its nose and quickly left the area, flying east toward the coast.

The gunships remained on-station and provided cover while those below completed the gruesome task of uncovering and searching dead enemy bodies, collecting weapons, and confiscating anything else of importance. Time was of the essence, especially if those who got away had any thought of returning with a larger force for some payback. Rock knew that he'd have to move his team to a new location once they completed their task and the overhead lights turned off.

The radio frequency remained unabated and free of traffic to accommodate Alpha Romeo 6.

"Thunder 3, this is Alpha Romeo 6, over."

"Roger, this is Thunder 3. Stand by for Bulldog 1, over."

"Wilco, standing by." There was a fifteen-second lull before someone spoke again.

LG held the radio handset between them so both he and Polack could listen to the conversation between Rock and the colonel.

"Alpha Romeo 6, this is Bulldog 1, can you give me an update, over?"

Rock was aware that Bulldog 1 was the battalion commander and knew from experience that he'd been waiting on pins and needles for his report. "Roger, Bulldog 1, we have nine NVA bodies, one an officer, collected seven AK-47 rifles, two Chicom pistols, a dozen or so full magazines and a few hundred loose rounds for both. All carried backpacks filled with personal items, food and a few grenades; the officer had a map and several other important-looking documents. This group also carried a base plate and tripod for an 82 mm mortar, several mortar rounds, but no tube, over."

"Excellent, Romeo 6, are you able to return with the equipment?"

"No sweat, Bulldog 1, we'll stuff anything looking important into a couple of the backpacks and divide everything else between us. We're leaving the bodies where they fell and burning the remainder of their supplies before leaving for the next location, over."

"Romeo 6, any idea where they might have come from?"

"We've got a pretty good idea, Bulldog 1. I'd guess they were part of the group that was responsible for the earlier mortar attack on the firebase. At least, I assume so, because of the base plate and rounds. It also looks like their approach was from that direction. I thought it was odd that they cut their way through the bush instead of following one of the trails, because they walked right into a mechanical that we set up in the jungle, but entered the kill zone from the opposite direction. We expected them to use the trail and placed one there in hopes of catching any soldiers who might try to escape in that direction after springing the ambush. Sometime during the firefight, some of them broke away and tripped one of the mechanicals we had placed on the trail east of our location. And I believe the rest of them escaped in that direction. There is a possibility that some may also be moving back toward the LP, over."

Polack and LG's eyes widened upon hearing that last point.

"Thank you, Romeo 6. I'm sorry about your wounded men and will see you all in the morning. Bulldog 1, out."

LG and Polack were surprised that only nine enemy soldiers perished during the ambush. 'Could it be that some perished during the earlier barrage to silence the tubes after they fired on the firebase?'

They continued their silent vigil, even more anxious now, knowing that enemy soldiers might be heading their way. Neither of them could see a thing, but continuously turned their heads in half-circles like personal radar, in an attempt to hear the slightest of sounds around them. The jungle was quiet; none of the creatures were making a sound. A chill ran down Polack's spine, causing his shoulders to hunch up, and he quickly shook his head when the shivers arrived. Nevertheless, he and LG were now wide awake and extremely vigilant.

The radio was devoid of conversation, only the rush of static remained until Rock later contacted the CP upon arrival at the alternate ambush site.

Try as he might, Polack was unable to prevent the tedium from taking its toll. Once again, he found his thoughts drifting back to other frightful experiences in his past.

ELEVEN - THE SISTER WITCHES

Passing my drivers exam and gaining access to the family car gave my pals and me an opportunity to travel outside of our neighborhood; we were anxious to investigate some of those stories told by our classmates who lived miles away and had to ride the bus to and from school.

One such opportunity presented itself just a couple of weeks after getting my license. It was a Friday night in mid-July, 1967. Four of us decided to visit an old home on the northeast border of Detroit, where it was said that two sisters - alleged witches - lived together. Many of those kids living nearby had confirmed that they were indeed evil, casting spells and doing other weird stuff. We'd been waiting a long time for this opportunity.

I was driving my dad's 1960 Ford Galaxy, en route to State Fair Rd. and Gratiot Rd., the intersection only one-half mile south of the suburbs. I parked the car a block away and our small group walked to the next corner.

The three-story old brick house stood tall on the next block. It looked to be over a hundred years old, and nothing else on the block came close in either age or size. The other homes were small ranches and bungalows built after the second World War.

Our destination looked like a replica of the Addams Family mansion, sitting on the second parcel from the corner. The corner and third lot were both empty fields of overgrown, head-high weeds and dozens of sunflowers. The plants poked up through the clumps of vegetation; their yellow and black heads swaying in the slight breeze, almost as if they were beckoning us to join them. Several extremely ancient weeping willow trees filled the property; long, drooping whips of leaves cascaded almost to the ground, hiding much of the house in shadows. A six-foot high black wrought iron fence surrounded the property; each vertical spoke as thick as a broomstick and sharpened on top like giant pencils. Needless to say, it would be a challenge for us to snoop around this spooky place.

A single street light illuminated the intersection, leaving the corner lot and beyond shrouded in shadow.

Wayne was the tallest in the group - a few inches over six feet - and the only one able to see above the tops of the vegetation, so he led the way. Paul and Ron followed nervously behind him, and I brought up the rear. Each of us was antsy; muscles felt poised and hardened, ready for action when needed. We moved ever so slowly through the jungle of weeds, keeping one hand on the shoulder of the person in front – the blind leading the blind toward the fence.

Once arriving, we stood next to the fence, holding onto the vertical bars while trying to get a good look at the side of the house and yard. There were several windows, but only two on the lower level glowed yellow from the light within. Spider webs covered the glass pane of the window on the left; small black orbs dotted the web in dozens of places.

"Looks like spiders living all over that web!" I moaned.

"I bet the witches are breeding those spiders and catching flies for their secret potions and shit," Wayne

declared and moved to the other side of us and away from the window. "I hate spiders!"

"So this is how inmates feel in a jail cell," Ron said in a facetious manner. He stood on the bottom cross bar and shook the fence to test its strength. "This thing is solid and might be a problem getting over."

"No, it won't," Paul interjected. "John and I scaled the fence at the cemetery, and it was much higher than this one. Right John?" Paul looked directly at me waiting for my concurrence.

"Yeah, we did, but that was different. We don't have a blanket now and can't see the ground on the other side. It'll be easy to get hurt jumping into that mess."

"Oh shit," Paul suddenly exclaimed and backed up a step or two, pointing to the right past Wayne. "Check out the tree in the back!"

We strained to see in the darkness, making out what looked like a big alley cat hanging by the neck from a rope. "That shit ain't real," Ron laughed, "it's got to be a prop or something."

"How do you know?" Paul asked.

"You smell anything?" Ron answered with a question of his own.

Paul raised his nose and took a few exaggerated sniffs of air. "No, not really," he admitted, shaking his head.

"Well, dead things rot and stink. That looks like a stuffed animal." Ron threw a stone at the suspended carcass, hitting it solidly in the side; none of them saw the stone fall. "See, it probably got trapped in the fake fur!" Ron boasted.

"I'm still not convinced."

"I'll show you." Ron scooted up the fence and perched there. He was about to jump over when he looked into the other lighted side window. Through the slight gap between the bottom of the drawn shade and the window, he could see shadows moving about inside. "Hey guys, check this out, there's somebody by the window. Maybe it's one of the witches!" he whispered.

We all looked up, nervous about what we might see. Ron, still sitting atop of the fence, slid to the right past a couple of the spears to get a better view. We couldn't see inside and awaited Ron's report.

Suddenly, we heard a loud flapping noise as the window shade shot upward and continued turning and clattering on the roller at the top of the window frame, exposing white lace curtains covered with embroidered flowers. Then all at once, a head popped up like a Jack in the Box and shrieked violently. It was the face of a witch – pointed nose, chin, warts and wispy gray hair covered by a black, wide brimmed pointed hat. She was missing most of her teeth, and her tongue lashed out at us.

Ron screamed first and launched himself from the fence, landing hard and then tumbling through the jungle of weeds. The rest of us were momentarily paralyzed and unable to react. Wayne was the first to come to his senses, pulling Paul and me with him as he began to run back toward the side street. We had almost made it when a police cruiser stopped at the intersection, then U-turned and pulled over to the curb on our side of the street. Wayne saw the car and pushed us to the ground just before two giant beams of light skimmed across the top of the bushes. Two officers stepped out of the car. "Anybody out there?" one called in a stern, authoritative voice. The two beams of light continued to crisscross over the field like spotlights at a Hollywood movie premier.

"Oh shit! What are we gonna do now?" Paul whispered anxiously, positioning his body flatter on the ground and holding his breath.

"Shh," I cautioned, "they don't know we're here." The ground was wet from an earlier rain, muddy in spots, and now that I was kneeling, my pant legs soaked up the moisture like a sponge. I wondered if the police officers could hear our hearts beating through the darkness. Mine was pounding in my ears.

Wayne was also on his hands and knees, his head swiveling left to right a few times before sitting back on his heels. He turned and looked to our left toward the alley. "Ron skipped out!" he whispered.

I looked to my left and was surprised to see him gone. "He was just here a minute ago," I gulped.

"Who's watching out for the witch?" Paul asked.

"I can't see shit from down here!" Wayne whispered.

Paul started to panic and tried to stand. "I'm giving up man. This hiding in the wet weeds shit ain't for me!"

Wayne and I both grabbed him by the arms and yanked him back down. "Stay the fuck down and be cool!" Wayne hissed.

"I'm scared, man," Paul implored, "I don't want to get into trouble over this. My folks will kill me!"

"We didn't do anything to get in trouble for," Wayne admonished. "Let's just wait and see what the man is gonna do next."

111

All at once, Ron emerged like a spooked partridge from a corner of the miniature jungle where the alley and side street met, then bolted down the middle of the street away from us and the police.

At the same time, we heard the cruiser doors slam; the single red chase light on the roof came to life, sending angry beams of pulsating light from the vehicle. Tires squealed, the smell of burning rubber wafted in the air. The squad car fishtailed as it sped down the side street after Ron.

The three of us jumped to our feet simultaneously, but only Wayne could see the road.

"Is the coast clear?" I asked anxiously.

"As far as I can see," Wayne responded.

"Where do you think he went?" Paul asked.

"No idea. Let's get back to the car!" I threw out.

"What about Ron?" Paul asked.

"He'll hook back up with us. Run!" Wayne commanded.

We ran like death was chasing us. Our wet pant legs added weight, impeding our speed. By the time we reached the car, I was shaking so badly that I couldn't get the key in the door lock to open it. Wayne and Paul were hollering almost hysterically, "Hurry!" which didn't help to calm me a bit.

"Come on man, they're gonna catch us!"

I threw the keys over the roof to Wayne, who quickly opened the passenger door, slid across the bench seat and opened both my door and the back for Paul.

"Now what?" I asked

"We can't just leave Ron. He'll show up here, so we gotta wait," Wayne said.

"What if the cops pull up? They'll nab us for sure," Paul questioned, his eyes nervously darting up and down the street.

"Just keep cool and relax," Wayne cautioned. "We'll give him fifteen minutes."

The sudden glare of headlights in the side-view mirror startled me. "Car coming, get the fuck down!" I shouted to the others.

Wayne and I slid down in the front seat, bending over sideways till the tops of our heads touched in the middle of the bench seat; Paul dove onto the rear seat floorboards. We waited patiently, praying the vehicle would pass without stopping, but something wasn't right - it was moving too slowly. I straightened and risked a quick look through the side mirror. "Shit!" I yelped, hitting the floor again. "It's the cops! They're driving real slow and checking both sides of the street with their spotlight."

"Keep cool and relax," Wayne warned, "and crack those windows a bit, they're starting to fog up!"

Wayne and I moved quickly, turning the hand crank a half turn to open the windows about a quarter. Not hearing a response from the back seat, Wayne ordered again, "Paul, crack the windows back there!"

"I can't move, man. I'm stuck!" came a muffled voice from behind the front seat.

The police cruiser was only a couple of houses back, its searchlight scouring the shrubbery and porches on both sides of the street, and moving forward at a crawl. A beacon of light radiated through our car several times during the sweeps back and forth across the road. The three of us held our breath, watching, hoping, and praying as the shadows danced through our car's interior. Once the cruiser was ahead of us, the light show stopped but we were still afraid to move.

"Did they stop?" Paul questioned in a nervous whisper.

"I don't think so, but I can't tell. Quiet now!"

"Listen," Wayne announced. "The engine noise and exhaust is fading away. They've passed!"

Breathing a sigh of relief, I shimmied up for a peek - just to verify - and saw that the squad car was now three houses down. "We're cool for now. They're almost at the end of the block."

Suddenly, a rapid banging against the passenger window interrupted the quiet. A large shadow blocked any light that entered through the glass. It startled us, prompting a loud, simultaneous shriek from the three of us. I mean, a shrill, high-pitched, girl-like scream emitted from our car.

"Guys, quit screaming like bitches and open the fucking door!"

Wayne quickly unlocked the back door, and Ron jumped in head-first sprawling across the back seat, landing right on top of Paul.

"Ron, how…!" I started.

"Help!" Paul choked. "I'm stuck and can't breathe!"

I pulled up the lever on the side of the front seat, and then Wayne and I shifted our bodies forward to move the bench seat closer to the dashboard. Ron reached down and pulled Paul up by his belt, freeing him to breathe again.

"I'll tell ya later. Right now, let's start this piece of shit and get the hell out of here!"

I started the car and made a three-point turn, racing to the end of the block and then turning south onto Gratiot Rd. toward home. Our heavy breathing was the only sound heard for the next five minutes.

"So you all screamed just like chicks back there. Wait until I let everyone know," Ron broke the silence and giggled.

Protests arose from the three of us, threatening Ron with multiple dismemberments if he were to squeal on us. Then just like that, we all broke into boisterous laughter, so hard and continuous that I had to pull over to the curb.

"What happens when we can't run anymore?" Paul gasped.

"Then the devil catches you and takes you to Hell," Wayne hollered above the loud guffaws.

"Are we going back to check out the witches' house tomorrow night?" Ron asked.

"Are you crazy?" Paul challenged.

Ron looked over at him and grinned. "Nope! We need to get a better look next time!"

"Not this guy," I called out from the driver's seat. "I couldn't survive another night like this one!"

"I'm sitting the next one out, too," Paul said. "I know I'm going to hurt tomorrow as it is. I probably have bruised ribs, and blisters on my feet."

"I'll go back with you!" Wayne volunteered, reaching into the back seat so Ron could slap his hand to seal the deal.

"Well then, it's you and me, brother."

If Wayne and Ron ever did go back, they never shared the adventure with the rest of us. I often wondered if their

115

spoken plan to return was just an act of bravado in front of Paul and me. Clearly, we all had the shit scared out of us that night.

Although I remained baffled about exactly what it was that we did see that dark night, it wasn't until years later that I found out the truth about the "Sister Witches".

While at my ten-year high school class reunion, my classmates and I were laughing and reminiscing - as people often do - about all of the crazy mischief we had gotten into during our adolescent years. I happened to mention our spooky night of "witch hunting", when one of the women at our table spoke up,

"Oh, don't tell me that you were one of the kids that fell for the Dombrowski sisters' prank?"

"...The Dombrowski sisters??" I said, not comprehending.

"Sure...I would have thought that urban legend bit the dust and was forgotten about years ago..." she smiled.

"Well, I..." I stammered, unwilling to admit that I had not yet figured out one of the most notorious mysteries of the old neighborhood.

She continued with a chuckle.

"Yeah, good ol' Agnes and her sister Helen must've gotten a lot of good belly laughs out of that joke. I guess it even made the local papers. It seems that they both got tired of all of the neighborhood rumors about them being witches, and they finally got fed up with all the kids snooping around their place at night... so they made a couple of really ugly witch masks... Any time they noticed kids doing the Peeping Tom thing, they'd wait until their victims got close enough,

then they'd get the masks on, and would throw up their shade and scare the crap out of 'em. Even the police felt sorry for those ladies; there were so many kids hanging around there at night that they'd patrol their street regularly, just to shoo 'em away. It got to be quite a thing."

All I could do was smile weakly and slowly nod in agreement, as though I, too, had been in on the hoax the whole time... I hoped my red face did not betray how clueless I'd been!

Still, I will never forget the pounding of my heart and the crushing surge of adrenaline that coursed through my body as we hid in the bushes that night. Little did I know that just two short years later, I'd find myself once again hiding in thick vegetation, hoping and praying to not be discovered. The next time, however, I'd be ten thousand miles from home in a foreign country, unable to run away, and one wrong move could mean certain death.

TWELVE - LISTENING POST (0200 HOURS)

It was almost 0300 hours when Alpha Romeo 6 reported to the CP that his group arrived at its new location and were hunkering down until daybreak. His route of travel was unknown, but it was clear that they didn't encounter any enemy soldiers while moving stealthily through the darkness.

Polack had the sudden realization, *'If they moved halfway between us and their first ambush site, then they're much closer to us, probably only within 500 meters.'* He looked at LG and formed the 'OK' sign, to which LG acknowledged with a single nod of his head. *'LG must be thinking the same thing. Now we can relax a little.'*

He sat back and rested against the tree trunk, feeling more content now that a squad of fellow soldiers was near and could respond within minutes if help was needed.

'This shit is still fucked up!' LG said to himself while moving around some to ease the numbness in his behind. *'How could my ass fall asleep and stay numb through all this tension?'* LG continued scooting around in hopes of finding his earlier comfort zone and waking his ass up. His left ear felt like it was burning, and his hands cramped, both due to his continuous monitoring of the radio.

Suddenly, from a distance to their front, they heard the sound of twigs breaking and brush being pushed aside. Both men simultaneously reacted to this new threat, sitting up straight, probing the darkness for signs of the intruder. The noise was intermittent, and the distinct sounds of small branches snapping and foliage rustling came and went as if somebody took two steps forward then waited for a few seconds before continuing. The two LP soldiers soon realized they were both holding their breath again for the umpteenth time. One thing was certain, whatever it was, it was moving straight toward them.

Polack slowly reached down, grabbed a grenade from the ground, and stuck his forefinger into the safety ring. He held it with both hands against his chest, getting ready to yank out the pin and throw the explosive baseball. At the same time, LG removed the safety on the firing device for the Claymore that covered their front, and, holding it firmly in hand, prepared to squeeze the device and trigger the mine. The movement was still out of effective range, but when triggered, the explosion would stop the enemy cold without giving up their position.

The two sat frozen to the spot. Their heads were still and facing straight ahead, but cocked slightly, straining to hear better. Both fixated on that sightless spot within the tunnel of darkness and - at this point - only trusted their sense of hearing. Nervous and sweating profusely, moisture pooled around Polack's neckline, gravity sending small rivulets of water racing down his back. His body, reacting in kind, sent chills back up his spine, a tingling shiver occurring every time the signal reached his brain.

The beating of their hearts tripled, allowing adrenaline to move through their veins at supersonic speed. Muscles flexed in anticipation of the approaching boost of energy, and large bass drums kept pace with the system, beating loudly in their ears. Both wondered if the intruder could hear them.

Another crash startled them, the threatening noise continuing its trek in their direction. LG quickly depressed the talk button on the handset twice to alert everyone that they might be in trouble.

An instant later, a voice whispered through the handset receiver. It was so quiet that Polack was unable to hear a single word, but knew from experience what was said.

"This is Thunder 3, unit in trouble. Please respond, over!"

LG remained quiet.

Everyone's curiosity was piqued and all waited anxiously for word from the field. After several more seconds, the same voice returned.

"This is Thunder 3," the CP radio operator again whispered,

"Lima Papa 1, sit rep." He started calling the field patrols on the checklist that he used every hour, trying to identify the team that was unable to talk.

LG responded by breaking squelch twice. The CP radio operator looked upward offering thanks that he succeeded in identifying them on the very first try.

"Roger, Lima Papa 1, please confirm a threat."

LG squeezed the talk button twice again in response.

"Roger Lima Papa 1, Thunder 3 standing by. Break...Break...Break, all units, unless there is an emergency, please keep this channel clear of traffic. Thunder 3, out."

All the other RTO's in the battalion knew the routine and would not broadcast until receiving clearance from the

CP operator. Meanwhile, all ears within the vicinity were glued to their receivers; the radio operators keeping those listening abreast of the situation.

'What the fuck is out there?' The crashing sound continued.

'I wish I could see!' LG was literally shaking in his boots.

'It's got to be those missing NVA soldiers that escaped from Rock's ambush. Sons of bitches are coming right for us,' Polack's brain warned him. He was also aware that a well-used trail separated their hiding place from the commotion and noise to their front. *'By the sound of it, they haven't hit the trail yet.'*

Then, with only ten feet of jungle remaining before reaching the hard-packed dirt trail, the noise stopped for good. It was still and quiet. The silence, deafening! *'Why did the enemy point man stop the column?'*

As the minutes ticked by, Polack and LG wished for a sighting, voices, or a wild boar's grunts to identify what they were facing. Unlike the earlier situation when the enemy stopped nearby for a break, this time there was no chatter, movement through the brush, toilet breaks, or the sound of foliage being crushed as soldiers dropped in place. Five minutes later, the suspense completely unnerved both men and they broke protocol to communicate in hushed voices.

"What's your take on this?" Polack whispered into his partner's ear.

"Ain't no telling!" LG responded.

"I think there's a column of NVA out there." Polack paused. "Do you think they have a Starlight Scope? I bet they're looking right at us and watching to see what we do."

"Damn, Polack! You're freaking me out! But it's too dark in this triple canopy, and a scope wouldn't help them anyway."

"Then why do you think they stopped?"

"Don't know, brother."

Once again, a slight rustling sound occurred in the brush where the movement had ceased earlier.

"Shhhh! Did you hear that?"

LG nodded in the affirmative. Both sat shoulder-to-shoulder and continued scanning the area before them.

After several more seconds, they heard a noise speeding through the overhead foliage, heading their way. Something landed just to their right with a crash like a metal shot put; the ground responded with a loud grunt.

'GRENADE!', the realization hit; the two men's brains screamed urgently and silently. Aware of the imminent danger, both fought their fear and jumped to their feet. Polack instinctively pulled the pin on the grenade, heaving the metal ball out to his front before joining LG in a disjointed dive into the brush on their left, away from the threat. Landing in a heap on the hard ground, they quickly covered their heads and assumed a fetal position. The outbound grenade's explosion sounded on the other side of the trail. No screams, and no sound of anyone vacating the area, but also no explosion from the enemy grenade that landed nearby.

'Dud grenade?'

After several seconds passed, both men cautiously raised their heads and glanced back toward their former location.

"Dud?" Polack asked.

123

Before LG could answer, another projectile landed to their left, prompting another evacuation - this time to the right - landing them back near their LP post. Again, no explosion. Both men looked at one another in bewilderment. LG asked the question that was currently spooling through their heads:

"What's the chance of two duds in a row?"

Polack didn't hesitate. He armed another grenade and lobbed it as far as he could, aiming blindly into the night. When that explosion again proved fruitless, their eyes searched through the darkness for their attacker, hoping he might inadvertently give away his hiding position. It was, however, impossible to see anything, try as they might. Suddenly, a third projectile landed on the ground, very close to the same spot where the first one landed. Once again, the men went airborne and dove into the thicket on their left. The seconds ticked by, and the men were astonished at the lack of an explosion for the third time.

"What the fuck is going on?" Polack demanded in a hushed tone. Stealth was no longer of importance, as the sounds of their crashing evasive actions and exploding grenades revealed their exact location to all – especially to whoever was toying with them.

"I don't know, bro. This shit is a first for me."

"Quick, let's each grab a grenade and toss it where we think they might be before they throw another one at us."

Without delay, they each pulled the pins and heaved the bombs out to their front before dropping on their bellies to hug the ground. Two back-to-back explosions sounded with such force that dirt and shrubbery rained down on the two men.

They remained prone, awaiting a response from their attackers. Smoke rose into the air; the latest explosions ignited small fires in the same area. The smell of cordite and burning vegetation permeated in their nostrils.

After a full minute, both heard Rock's voice calling from the radio handset,

"Lima Papa 1, this is Alpha Romeo 6, over."

LG groped around, looking for the handset, using Rock's voice as a guide to locate it. He found it just as Rock completed his second call.

"This is Lima Papa 1. Go ahead, Romeo 6, over." LG was gasping during his response, out of breath from the physical workout.

"What is your status?" Rock asked. "Do you need help?"

"Negative. Our sit-rep is green at the moment. We heard movement in our front, and then within minutes, three grenades landed in our position. We had to evade and are both okay, over."

"We heard four explosions," Rock responded. "Where did they come from?"

"Uh…the three enemy grenades appeared to be duds. The four explosions you heard were from our grenades, over."

There was a slight delay before Rock responded, a bit louder this time.

"Roger, Papa 1. You mean to tell me that whoever was out there threw three grenades at you and all three were duds?"

"Affirmative, over."

"Have you confirmed the presence of these three dud grenades?"

"Negative, it's too dark to look for them."

Just then, a large whining screech sounded from the treetops above them. It began with a shrill scream, then evolved into a hum that dropped down the musical scale until it reached a deep bass tone, continuing at that level for a few more seconds before stopping. After a brief delay, another loud screech gave an encore of the same performance.

"Lima Papa 1, is that an animal call nearby?"

"Roger, Romeo 6. It seems to be coming from the same area where we had all the movement."

Once again, Rock was silent for a moment. The CP radio operator broke in before Rock could speak again.

"Break, break, Lima Papa 1, this is Thunder 3, over." The voice sounded tense and with a slight hint of irritation.

LG looked at Polack and whispered,

"Uh-oh. Sounds like somebody in the CP is pissed."

Polack shook his head,

"I'm hip, bro."

He positioned himself to listen in on the shared receiver while LG talked.

"Ah, this is Lima Papa 1, go ahead, Thunder 3."

"Roger, Lima Papa 1. Bulldog 1 wants to know if you saw enemy soldiers or did you respond only to the movement. Over."

"This is Lima Papa 1. The sound was moving toward us and then stopped about thirty feet to our front. It was quiet for five minutes, then grenades started landing in our position. All three projectiles failed to detonate, and while taking evasive action, we returned fire by tossing grenades back at them. Over."

"This is Bulldog 1," his voice a deep baritone, yet sincere and father-like. "Understand that you took evasive action on what turned out to be three dud enemy grenades and then responded with grenades of your own in retaliation? Am I correct?"

"Affirmative, Bulldog 1."

"But you haven't been able to verify the existence of the dud grenades and hadn't received weapons fire from the suspected enemy?"

"Affirmative, Bulldog 1."

"...Okay, son... I think there's a lesson to be learned here."

He chuckled before he continued, "I think the shriek you heard moments ago came from your attacker."

"Say again, Bulldog 1. The sound we heard wasn't human."

The men shifted uncomfortably and wondered what the colonel was getting at.

"This is Bulldog 1. Have you ever encountered apes or monkeys in the bush?"

Polack shook his head side to side.

"Uh, negative, Bulldog 1."

"Monkeys and Rock Apes are highly territorial. Males throw things to show dominance over other creatures. In your case, I'd be willing to bet that a male of the species wanted you to move out and threw rocks to intimidate you so you'd leave. And since four grenades didn't silence him, chances are he dropped them from the treetops directly above you."

LG and Polack were at a total loss for words. When LG finally found his voice, he was only able to utter a single word,

"O...kay."

The colonel returned after a moment. "I still want to commend you for taking the initiative to engage towards a potential threat. I will caution you, though, to continue your vigilance. The enemy is still out there. Bulldog 1, out."

The two men, mortified, were silent for a few moments.

"Folks are going to come down on us big time in the morning," LG sighed, before settling comfortably back against the small tree for the last hour and a half of their shift.

"I hear you, LG. But fuck 'em all!"

"Dat's right! None of the other brothers in the company would have acted any different. But just to be safe, we should keep this between you and me. No use giving anybody a reason to get into our shit."

Polack followed LG's lead and returned to his lookout position against the second tree.

"Here it comes!" he muttered.

Only five minutes passed before the CP began another round of calls for sit-reps, as the clock read 0400 hours.

"Lima Papa 1, sit-rep," Thunder 3 called.

Instead of clicking once, LG responded,

"This is Lima Papa 1. Since everyone knows we're out here now, we're requesting permission to return to the firebase, over."

"This is Thunder 3, negative on your return. Remain in position, keep your eyes open... and watch out for falling rocks! Out. Lima Papa 2, sit-rep..."

"Cocksucker!" both men exclaimed at the same time.

"They think this shit is funny. I wonder how they'd feel being in our boots."

"Don't mean nothin', LG. Let it go, man!"

He thought about it for a second or two,

"Yeah, you right, bro'! But I'm telling ya' right now that if another rock or whatever lands nearby, I'm outta here!"

"I'll be right behind ya', bud!"

As the adrenaline drained from their bodies, both men began to shake as violently as if they were sitting in a blizzard in the middle of winter without a coat. The lack of sleep was also taking its toll. Both were drowsy and fought hard to stay awake and, more importantly, to remain alert.

There was a little more than an hour to go before they could break camp and return to the firebase. Both were looking forward to a hot breakfast, coffee, and sleep, in that order.

Polack continued to shiver and thought back to another childhood experience when he needed to act in spite of his fear.

THIRTEEN - BELLE ISLE: SWIMMING IN THE RIVER

Belle Isle is a small island in the middle of the half-mile wide Detroit River, located between the shores of downtown Detroit and Windsor, Ontario, Canada. The island has a notorious background including its usage as a loading point for bootleggers, ferrying alcohol from Canada during Prohibition. One obtained access to the island by crossing over a quarter-mile long bridge from the east shore of Detroit, unless of course, one has a boat; several marinas with docks could moor any size watercraft. In 1906, it was from this very same bridge that the famed magician, Harry Houdini, attempted a dangerous trick called the "Overboard Packing Box Escape". For the performance, Houdini was tied and handcuffed inside of a wooden box. The box was then nailed and tied shut with overlapping ropes. Finally, with Houdini inside, the crate was lowered through a hole in the ice of the river. Houdini had mere seconds to escape from both the restraints and the box. The myth we all heard while growing up in the old neighborhood was that Houdini had drowned in these waters during a similar failed stunt, but in reality, his trick was a success and a nearby boat picked him up. He died twenty years later in 1926.

The residents of Detroit came to this island for relaxation and to escape the heat and stresses of big city living. During a summer weekend, the beaches, picnic areas, athletic fields, zoo, aquarium, and flower gardens overflowed with visitors.

As an alternative to visiting the crowded public places, many people simply cruised the loop around the island, driving slowly to enjoy the cool island air. The panorama of freshly manicured lawns, ornamental flower beds lining the road, and lovers paddling canoes through the many internal canals were enough to tranquilize the senses.

It was common to see families either sitting on blankets at the shoreline or sitting in parked cars on the side of the road. Everyone watched in awe as giant lake freighters and pleasure boats passed by in both directions.

For families of modest means - such as mine - Belle Isle offered the closest thing to a vacation they'd experience, and for many, it was their only frame of reference for the great outdoors.

In the early 1960's, our family lived only a few blocks away from the Belle Isle bridge. During the summer months, my friends and I spent every sunny day on the island. As preteens, we either bummed a ride or walked to the beach. Being fearless and feeling invincible, we sometimes ended up doing stupid things that appeared to be an adventure at the time.

We usually spent our days at the boathouse adjacent to the beach. The wooden docks rose five feet above the water and extended beyond a line of barrels, marking a boundary for swimmers. Water depths at the dock's end were eight to ten feet. Nearby lifeguards allowed swimmers to jump and dive from them; wooden ladders made it easy for swimmers to climb out of the water for a repeat performance. Here, the riverbed was "mushy" and covered with seaweed. One

132

of our in-group challenges was to see who could jump the deepest into the muck below; the texture was like melted clay and left telltale prints on our legs, coating them with a mixture of goop that remained until we scraped it off with a stick or flat stone, making it easy to determine the winner.

We had all experienced going too deep into the muck and getting stuck on occasion. Panic stricken, we'd claw at the seaweed and try desperately to escape from the suction imprisoning us. It seemed like the more we panicked, the more difficult it was to get free. We couldn't use our hands to push off from the bottom because of the mucky texture. Through trial and error, we soon learned that if we relaxed and tried to crawl along the bottom, we could pull ourselves free and rise to the top.

I do remember one time when one of us got into trouble and almost drowned. Michael Tomas, the youngest and skinniest of the group, jumped in and wasn't coming back up. We stood there on the deck waiting for him to surface and watched the water for signs. When a stream of bubbles burst to the surface, the three of us jumped in without hesitation. Michael had trapped himself in slime beyond his knees but he was conscious when we managed to pull him free and get him back onto the dock. Thankfully, he was still breathing. It was a good thing, too, because none of us guys were willing to give him mouth-to-mouth resuscitation! We all laughed about the incident later, but the lifeguard wasn't pleased. He expelled us from the docks, thus ending our day of swimming.

Another time, a construction company was repairing the bridge by working from a floating platform on the river. They had constructed scaffolding on the raft extending fifty feet up to the underside of the arched structure. The platform, anchored about the same distance from the seawall, sat on the city side of the river, in front of the massive Wonder Bread Company monument; a three-story replica of an antique black iron kitchen stove which faced Jefferson Avenue.

We had no idea of the water's depth but thought it would be cool to swim out to the platform and dive from the scaffolding. We agreed that one of us had to stay behind with a rope to help the others climb back up the seawall, since no ladder was mounted anywhere nearby. We drew blades of grass to determine the loser; the shortest stayed behind. Michael lost - or won - depending on how you look at it.

We weren't aware that the city dredged the clay river bottom here, or that the current was treacherous. Unfortunately, we discovered this the hard way. We were all strong swimmers for 12 year-old boys, as we participated on the local Boy Scout swimming team. Having regularly dove into the river from various heights on the island side, the eight-foot high seawall didn't intimidate us. However, when the three of us jumped into the water together, the current immediately took hold of us and pulled us away from the floating scaffold. We swam with all our might, but didn't make any progress in closing the distance. Our efforts matched the speed of the current and only kept us stationary at a point of no return, halfway between the shore and the raft.

Michael, already in panic mode, paced back and forth along the seawall with a twenty-foot long rope. It wasn't long enough to reach us, but if we could swim to it, then

Michael could help us up. I tried to tell Patrick and James about my idea, but the waves lapping against my face made me gag while attempting to get the words out.

Finally, I relayed the message using pantomime: pointing to the rope in the water, and hollering, "ROPE" several times. They acknowledged and began making their way in that direction. Michael kept pace with them as the current moved them away from the bridge and along the seawall.

I saw nothing to grasp along the seawall and figured that three of us trying to reach the rope would actually make it harder for us to get out. I focused on the raft instead, burying my face in the water and swimming as if I were participating in one of our weekly races in the high school's swimming pool.

The current relinquished its death grip on me once I moved farther from shore. This reprieve allowed me to swim toward the bridge and then approach the floating platform from behind. I saw a ladder mounted on an attached platform; it was used to unload and store supplies for the much larger stationary raft. I summoned the last of my strength and swam the final twenty feet toward salvation. Snatching the lowest rung, I held on tightly as the small raft bobbed up and down in the water, behaving like a bronco bull trying to throw me off. It was now or never.

I managed to pull myself up and fell onto the bobbing platform. My muscles spasmed, my lungs were on fire, and my ribs screamed in pain as they all expanded to accommodate every deep, gulping breath. Feeling dizzy, I knew I was hyperventilating from the whole experience. Trying to control my breathing, I exhaled into my clasped fists, using it like a paper bag. My two friends still struggled in the water. They held on to Michael's dangling rope like landed fish hanging at the end of a storage line. Energy expended, neither had enough strength to pull himself up the eight-foot high seawall. Confident that they were safe for the moment, I relaxed momentarily. However, the constant bobbing brought on a case of motion sickness. I bent over the side and hurled my earlier breakfast into the water, watching the regurgitated glob of cereal, pancakes, and bile move downriver away from me. I prayed that my friends didn't see me as it would definitely hurt my image.

Suddenly, I spotted a police car driving over the top of the slope above Michael, heading directly toward him. Michael waved frantically to get the officer's attention, but they were already well aware of us. Looking up for the first time, I noticed groups of people gathered on the bridge above, all watching us, many exhibiting looks of sheer terror on their faces. The ladies bit their fists and the men held their partners tightly in their arms. Somebody up there had called the police.

To make matters worse, a small Coast Guard vessel manned with four officers arrived on the scene. The captain fought the current and held the boat stationary while two Coasties pulled Patrick and James into the craft. A medic checked them over while the cruiser motored toward me to pluck me from the bobbing platform. Spectators on the bridge clapped and cheered - a near disaster avoided. They continued watching the vessel as it moved slowly across the river toward the island.

The Coasties were extremely kind. They covered us with wool blankets and appeared genuinely concerned about our well-being. The three of us were excited and agreed that this was turning out to be one great adventure so far.

After we tied off at the Coast Guard Station, we saw Michael standing near the dock with two police officers, our clothes and shoes sitting in a pile at his feet. Michael was crying. Thin rivulets of tears created trails running down his dust-encrusted face; they dripped onto his shoes from the edge of his chin. The look on his face gave us pause. Michael was not a weak person and seldom cried. Maybe the police officers told him that he would go to jail for his part in what they now called a prank.

We began to worry while drying off and redressing in our crumpled clothes. Why were the police officers still hanging around? We didn't do anything wrong! We were just on an adventure, challenging ourselves – and each other – to try something new.

Once we were dressed, the police officers escorted the four of us to an office containing a long table and a dozen chairs. After taking their seats, the officers eyeballed each of us, shaking their heads in disgust. None of us dared move; fear kept us frozen to the spot. This adventure was no longer fun.

The officers greatly intimidated us. They threatened us with a stint in a juvenile detention facility and hundreds of dollars in fines for doing something so stupid. Petrified, we shivered uncontrollably. Needless to say, none of us wanted to be taken away from our homes, and we had no money to pay the fines. We started crying, promising that we would never do anything like that again, but they weren't listening to us and just tuned us out.

When they told us that our parents were telephoned, informed about our stupid stunt, and were on their way to pick us up, we freaked out! Fighting the river currents wasn't that big of a big deal to us, and in our naiveté, none of us were truly scared during the ordeal; it was more of an adrenaline rush… a real adventure. The reality of drowning never entered our minds. However, real fear surfaced when the four of us thought about what our parents would do to us when we got home. The anticipation of the unknown had its way with me, and the first of many future panic attacks began. It's unfortunate that they had to start at such a young age.

Our parents soon filed in, first smothering us with hugs and kisses for not dying, then subjecting themselves to a severe tongue-lashing from the head police officer. They remained humbled and were not defensive. Instead, they exhibited respect and patience while waiting until they could take us home. The officers released us to the custody of our parents and did not press charges. Four separate cars exited the Coast Guard Station parking lot and merged into the bridge traffic returning to the city.

My parents didn't say a single word on the drive home. Dad's face was red and stern, his mind trying to sort through these recent events. He glanced at me a few times in the rear-view mirror, but I knew better than to say anything. When we arrived home, I didn't want to get out of the car. I felt safe from the reach of my parents while still in the car with the doors locked. When Dad saw that I wasn't getting out, he returned, opened the door and looked in with an angry look on his face, then growled, "Into the house, Mr. Olympic Swimmer." He didn't smile or mean it as a joke. I hesitated, still unsure if I should or shouldn't move. Dad lost his patience and shouted, "NOW!" His voice alarmed me enough to launch me out of the car. I ran as fast as my legs could carry me, taking the porch steps two at a time, and then dashing through the open front door in a blur. I continued straight to my bedroom, slammed my door, and propped my desk chair under the doorknob to keep them out. When my father banged on the door and yelled my name repeatedly, my lack of response didn't fool him into thinking that I wasn't there. After a couple more hard knocks with his fist and wild jostling of the handle, the door suddenly burst open. Dad stepped into my room, swinging his brown leather belt from his right hand.

Yeah, I was punished, big time. My parents forbade me to go to Belle Isle for the rest of the summer, doling out additional chores and confining me to my room for the next two weeks. Of course, I didn't have a computer, video games, or a cell phone to pass the time - those inventions were still decades away - leaving me with only an AM radio and my comic books for company. I didn't see my buddies, Michael, Patrick or James until the first day of school at the beginning of the following month. It seemed like the parents collaborated because all of our punishments were similar.

Oh, and I should add that when I left for Vietnam, I still had the welts running across my ass from where dad's leather belt roasted my flesh only six years earlier. The whole misadventure of diving under the bridge, turned out to be a foolish and painful experience.

But... I have to confess... what a rush it was!

FOURTEEN - LISTENING POST (0400 HOURS)

The 04:00 litany of sit-reps concluded moments ago; all units responded with single breaks in the static, thus assuring battalion CP that everyone was awake and all was secure.

Polack and LG still struggled with the mosquitoes that plagued them since their arrival the previous evening. Both soldiers remained cocooned in their poncho liners with only their eyes peeking through a slight gap in the material. They blocked out the incessant buzzing around their ears, passing it off as something beyond their control. Like tinnitus, the irritable sounds become accepted as part of the normal hearing process. Periodically, one of them would either spit or blow air through a nostril to dislodge an errant insect that made it through their defenses.

It was exceptionally silent; the only sound was the breeze blowing through the overhead canopy. The relaxing noise made it easy to imagine sitting on a beach, listening to the palm fronds swaying in the breeze and hearing the waves gently roll onto the sand from the dark sea.

Any thoughts of paradise were interrupted as drops of rain began falling through the treetops above them. A sudden memory from training brought them out of their stupor. *'If you take care of your rifle, it will take care of you!'* As if their Drill Sergeant was standing right in front of them, both men raced to remove the small, clear cellophane wrappings from their C-Ration cigarettes, slipped them over their rifle barrel suppressors and secured them with rubber bands. The jungle humidity wrecked havoc on M-16's, so soldiers religiously cleaned and oiled them daily to keep them working properly. Even a single particle of rust or dirt in the right place could cause a misfire or jam.

The rain fell lightly at first, then grew in intensity as the minutes passed. It didn't take long for their poncho liners to absorb the moisture and transform into a much heavier wet blanket that leaked through, soaking them to the bone. Both pulled their rifles into the cocoons and hunkered down, careful not to dispel any of the warmth that the soaking wet liners provided.

After fifteen minutes, their shallow depression in the ground became almost intolerable. Water raced along the ground in several newly formed streams; the thin ribbons of mud flowed from the rim like miniature waterfalls. Without any outlet, the accumulated water quickly reached a depth of several inches. Ripples were beginning to roll over their thighs and crash into their bodies like those in a bathtub.

"Motherfuckin' rain!" Polack remarked, rising to his knees and leaning back against the trees to keep his ass out of the water. LG followed his lead a few seconds later. Neither was concerned about the grenades lying in the puddle of water. They were, however, anxious about the Claymore firing devices getting wet, because they required an electrical charge to detonate the mines, and neither knew if water hindered their operation. As a precaution, LG moved them out of the water to some higher ground.

Suddenly, the jungle brightened as lightning flashed overhead, and a loud clap of thunder startled the two men.

The rain fell harder, every drop causing geysers to splash up several inches in the growing pool. Thunder and lightning continued, without a break, which allowed them to see their surroundings for the first time that night. They didn't get a steady or clear picture. Instead, the light pulsated like a giant strobe, giving the impression that the surrounding trees and shrubbery were dancing in the shadows.

"This shit ain't right, brother! That lightning is freaking me out." LG announced, his voice quivering.

"I don't ever remember being in a storm like this before. My mother always told me to stay away from trees when there was lightning during a storm like this."

LG chuckled, "Yeah, mine too. If they only knew!"

Polack caught a whiff of something strange. "Hey, you smell that?" he asked.

"Yeah, smells like an electrical fire."

"Oh shit!" Polack exclaimed. "Get down!" He dove for the ground, pulling LG with him. Both belly-flopped into the small lake they were already sitting in.

"What the fuck?" LG raised his head, coughing and spitting mouthfuls of muddy water.

Polack put a hand on LG's head and forced it back down. "The Claymores, LG!"

As if on cue, two of the three mines to their front exploded, the sound much louder than the overhead thunder. Hundreds of steel balls blew outward into the foliage demolishing everything in their path for thirty feet. The eruption and back-blast created a small crater, its force sending the contents high into the air, then mixing with the raindrops as the debris fell back to earth and over the two prone soldiers. The telltale smell of cordite and raw earth began to mask the sharp electrical stench.

Suddenly, several more rapid explosions sounded from behind them at the firebase, all in close proximity of the LP.

"Shit must be contagious!" LG muttered, listening to the explosions around them. When they ceased, he rose from the water.

"Thanks, brother man! I didn't realize that was gonna happen!" He wiped the mud from his face and looked solemnly at Polack.

"I've seen it before..." Polack explained. "We had Claymores, detonation cord, and blasting caps explode during a storm right after I arrived. Shit, those little blasting caps will blow your fingers right off if they're triggered while you're holding them in your hand. In fact, I remember hearing something about that during our training."

LG shook his head, "I musta been sleeping that day!"

The lightning flashed and thunder clapped, but the storm seemed downgraded a couple of notches from ten minutes before.

"Oh, wow, man! Is the hair on your arms standing straight up?" LG asked, holding his arm up in front of his face.

Polack stroked his arm and confirmed the same.

"The static electricity from the storm is still in the air. We were lucky!"

"Yes, indeed!" LG declared.

Through all of this, LG still had the radio handset glued to his ear. The static electricity also affected the radio, as conversations were breaking up and the squelch seemed exceptionally loud.

"Anybody reporting anything?"

LG listened for a moment, then replied.

"Yeah, seems like Rock's group, LP Two, and one of the firebase bunkers had mines explode. Nobody got hurt, just scared the shit out of 'em all! Just like us!"

"Man, this is turning out to be one of my worst nights ever!" Polack watched LG for a reaction.

"I'm hip to that," he agreed. "Only another hour of this shit and we can di-di back to civilization."

"Yeah, you got that right!"

Polack sat down Indian-style on the rim of the water-filled depression. The storm had passed, but a steady light rain continued. Just one more hour to go… Content to see the light at the end of the tunnel, nothing else could dampen his spirits now. Polack hunched over and rested his arms on his knees to ease the strain on his back. The two men were exhausted mentally and physically. They were cold, wet, and hungry. Again Polack's thoughts began to ramble. As he relaxed a bit, he allowed them to take over, offering a mini-escape from his grim reality. A smile crossed his face as he thought back to another defining moment – an incident on Belle Isle that occurred only a couple of years earlier.

FIFTEEN - BELLE ISLE WOODS: INITIATION

When I was growing up, the woods on Belle Isle were always dark and mysterious. Sometimes, while driving through the shadowy forest, deer and other forms of wildlife made their presence known to those people who dared venture into their domain during daylight hours. The trees were a mixture of birch, elm, maple and spruce; some of them reached heights of 40 to 50 feet. Wild vines surrounded the tall trees and were tethered to their trunks; some wrapped around like a barbershop pole, reaching up from the ground to form a dense ceiling below the treetops. The brush was so thick it was near impossible to enter beyond twenty feet of the road. The canopy, lush and vibrant during the late spring, consequently blocked out both sunlight and moonlight from penetrating to ground level.

Felled timber, a result of old age, disease, or a windstorm, lay in a hodgepodge throughout, as if a giant spilled a container of Pick-up Sticks from the heavens. Carpenter ants and termites worked furiously, doing their part to eliminate these eyesores. Those ancient trees that remained standing would bend and sway in the breeze. The sound of rustling leaves carried through the moist air, along with the intermittent sounds of wood snapping, crackling and popping. At night, one might imagine the sound as coming from a group of men on foot moving wordlessly through the vegetation.

During the early spring months and after summer thunderstorms, much of the terrain remained wet and molding. Pools of stagnant water were everywhere; the cesspools served as havens and breeding grounds for mosquitoes and other insects. The thick humid air, carried the sharp scent of decay, rotting vegetation, and sewer-like smells. Most people weren't aware of the rancid odor because they didn't venture into the woods on foot during the day. Instead, visitors remained in their vehicles, only driving past the woods while on their way to the various attractions on the island.

Mosquitoes swarmed the woods and bit all summer long, day and night. Spiders thrived here, easily weaving their sticky webs between the tree limbs and the bushes down below. An occasional snake might be spotted sunning itself on the steaming black asphalt roads.

The island took on an entirely different aura at night, as teens ruled the night after families returned home. They'd gather in familiar areas of the island where they smoked, drank booze, necked in cars, or sat on the river shoreline to fish or watch the aquatic sights from park benches along the road.

On some nights, bonfires on the north side of the island lit the sky, signaling the location of a large party in the making, and all were welcome.

Smaller groups, comprised of students all from the same school, frequently kept to themselves. School rivalries were strong in certain neighborhoods, and on occasion, a brawl would erupt after one competing school group taunted the other. A huge rivalry existed between kids from the Catholic and public schools. Quite often, public school students underestimated the toughness of the private school kids, and many an ego was damaged in a rumble. Back then, they fought with chains, tire irons, two-by-fours, and knives. Guns were practically non-existent, and fighting during that time meant face-to-face, mano a mano. I even remember some of the Catholic school girls running around after a fight with handfuls of hair or blood on their knuckles as proof of their fighting prowess. It was also a time when "Greasers" and "Frats" reigned supreme in our teenage world; any derogatory remark between the groups was enough to spark a confrontation.

The island employed a small contingency of Detroit Police officers; most patrolled on horseback, but the understaffed force couldn't keep an eye on everyone.

In those frenzied high school years, accepting a challenge to hike through the woods after dark was a rite of passage. Money was sometimes wagered, but more importantly, reputations were at stake, and none of us wanted to be considered a "sissy" for the rest of the school year.

There were only two small, single-lane roads that snaked through the woods from the north and northeast side of the island. They sometimes intersected, crossing over small bridges suspended over a lagoon and narrow canals, eventually spitting you out on the other side, about a mile away, as the crow flies. A person could easily get disoriented while trekking through the darkness and might find himself going in circles because of a wrong turn. With no flashlights to light the way inside the pitch-black forest, visibility was fifteen to twenty feet, at best.

One late September night, a group of seniors from my high school intimidated me - a sophomore at the time - into making the trek through the woods. My buddy Wayne was along that night and volunteered to accompany me. I could never figure him out; it seemed like nothing ever scared that guy. At least, that's how it appeared on the surface. Wayne did not attend my school but knew most of the students from living in the same neighborhood. He was two years younger but towered over me by a good four inches. We were good friends and partners "in crime", doing everything together. In fact, I later joined him on many occasions as kind of a third wheel when he and his future bride, Doris, went out on dates. We went to the movies, drive-in diners, bowling, or just hung out, and sometimes I drove while they made out in the back seat. Never heard any shit over it later from either of them. We're still good friends today and laugh about it now and then.

The two of us stood at the mouth of the forest, shaking our hands and arms at our sides as if preparing for a major race in a large sporting event. Our peers supported us with slaps on the back and shouts of encouragement.

"It ain't shit! See ya' on the other side." Wayne and I smiled at Big Bob in acknowledgment.

"You can do it, John!" shouted a female classmate of mine.

"Right on, Barb! Thanks!" I responded, pumping my fist in the air.

Barb's confidence in me made my ego soar. She was a hippie chick with long, dark, straight hair that cascaded over her shoulders to the middle of her back. I sat behind her in a few classes and sometimes played with her hair and teased her a lot. She was bashful at times but was good-natured and took everything in stride.

Barb hung out with a clique of girls who were into rock and psychedelic music, and they spent their weekends at rock concerts. But what impressed me was that she shared my interest in creative writing. Her imagination, wit, and uncanny knack for details gave her a natural flair for the written word. Nothing got by her, and her mind was like a steel trap. Most of all, I liked that she laughed at all my goofy jokes – important stuff for a teen-age guy. I liked her; she was cute - but I never got the nerve to ask her out.

The upperclassmen also joined in with catcalls of their own. "Remember trolls and witches live under the bridges and they're gonna fuck you up when they catch you!" Billy needled. The tall blond senior and basketball star exhibited a shining white smile that reminded me of the then-popular jingle in Pepsodent toothpaste commercials. Chills suddenly ran down my back causing me to shudder involuntarily. Tales of murderers, thieves, bums, and the ghost of The Great Houdini lurking in the eerie shadows compelled us to move cautiously through the dark abyss. Neither of us could see the white lines at the edge of the asphalt road, so kicking up stones or hearing the sound of crunching gravel was our only cue to move back on the road. Once we were out of the group's sight, we both armed ourselves with pieces of tree limbs about the size of a baseball bat, giving us a sense of some security.

Several youths often hid in the forest; their sole purpose was to spook the walkers. We weren't aware of this fact until weeks later. They were strangers to most and got their rocks off watching trekkers get freaked out. Rumors circulated about students actually passing out when accosted by this group during walk-throughs. As we passed by, they tossed stones at us, rustled through the vegetation, and moaned loudly like lost ghouls. Some were even stealthy enough to touch us, giving us a start, but we passed it off as just another event of nature and continued forward at a steady gait. Neither of us dared to run through this 'dark spook house' in fear of crashing straight into a tree or falling into one of the many canals. Our worst fear was that we might venture off the road into the brush, and become disorientated and unable to find our way back to the road.

We held on to one another's shoulders, single-file, while making our way forward. Occasionally, I found Wayne pushing me from behind but following closely in my footsteps. I never thought to ask if he was using me as a shield or trying to make me move faster.

The bridges were unique structures in that they were only twenty or so feet across, with an ornamental concrete barrier on both sides. The approach was not gradual, instead rising abruptly at a 45-degree angle to a height of four feet or so before they sharply sloped back down. During the daylight hours, teens raced their cars through the woods intent on going airborne when reaching the bridges. Many of the cars bottomed out, leaving deep grooves and ruts in the asphalt where the transmission, engine oil pan, or frame hogged out pieces of the road. Others crashed their vehicles; telltale signs like damaged tree trunks or car pieces laying in the brush on the side of the road were all that remained as remembrances of somebody's stupidity.

We soon came to the first of two bridges that we had to cross before taking a dogleg to the right. It was almost midnight, and we'd been on the move for more than an hour already. For some reason, we stopped, both overcome with a sense of dread. Trolls and witches are real! I knew this for a fact, having learned all about them at summer camp and from the stories Carmen's mother told us. I even saw a real witch myself at the Sister Witches house! Wayne must have had his own reasons for remaining rooted to the spot; I'm sure his imagination was working overtime, as well.

We heard some scraping sounds coming from under the bridge, much like someone dragging a rock across concrete. Then a loud splash as something heavy fell into the water, followed by the sounds of deep guttural grunting and high-pitched cackling.

Wayne elbowed me in the side.

" What was that?!"

Whispering, I said, "It must be the trolls and witches!"

Wayne sounded astonished,

"Aw, that's all bullshit! Urban legends!"

"Well, what do you think is happening then?"

"I think somebody's fucking with us and trying to scare us or trap us on the bridge."

"Well, they sure got my full attention!" I stated, unsure as to how we should proceed. "What now?"

Wayne started to move around and shuffled his feet across the asphalt.

"Let's look for something to throw," he suggested.

I began exploring the dark, damp earth, hoping to come across something worthwhile. I stubbed my toe against a cantaloupe-sized object. Reaching down, I found what I thought to be a car headlamp. At least, it sure felt like one.

Moving back toward Wayne, I whispered loudly,

"Wayne, where are you? I found a headlamp!"

He responded from the bushes on the side of the road,

"I'm right here, Partner! Keep talking so I can find you."

I continued chatting nonsense until Wayne reached my side.

"What's the plan?" I asked.

"I found some good-sized rocks over there. I've got four in my hands and a couple more in my pockets." Wayne then placed two of the apple-sized stones into my hand. "We're going to throw these rocks at each side of the bridge to see what comes out. If punk-ass kids are under there, then these will bring them out."

"Then what?"

"We take our clubs and run."

"What if it's not kids?"

"Same thing, only faster."

We each chose a side and threw a single rock, aiming slightly to the side of the bridge. Wayne's rock hit a tree, and the sudden sharp 'CRACK!' startled us. It sounded like one of the Detroit Tigers had just hit a home run. My rock hit the water on the opposite side with a resounding splash a few seconds later. The scraping sound and other ungodly noise from under the bridge immediately stopped.

"Throw again!" Wayne whispered.

This time, his rock landed in the water, and my headlamp bounced through some shrubbery near the canal.

"What the fuck was that?!" someone questioned from the shadows below. The voice was a male, and it sounded strained.

"There's something on this side, too!" another voice commented, sounding spooked. Suddenly, the powerful beam of a flashlight lit up the canal on the right side of the bridge and darted through the foliage.

"Run!" Wayne whispered, shoving me forward, making sure to keep a hand on my shoulder while following close behind. The flashlight beam continued searching for us on both sides of the bridge, which provided just enough light to cross the bridge and safely reach the dogleg. Those underneath never saw us.

When total darkness enveloped us once again, we stopped to catch our breath.

"Told you it was just some punk-ass kids!" Wayne threw out in between labored breaths. I could only acknowledge his comment with a head-shake as my mouth was too busy sucking in oxygen.

We didn't have far to go now. The second bridge was at the end of the dogleg. After crossing that, we'd be in the clear. The road continued with the woods bordering on the left and a nine-hole golf course encompassing the right. A gaggle of students usually gathered where this street merged into the main perimeter road near the beach.

Our moment of self-congratulations evaporated when a bright flash of lightning followed by a loud clap of thunder ushered in a chilly Autumn storm. The rain fell suddenly and hard, completely soaking us before even taking a step.

"This blows!" I grumbled.

"Yeah, but look at the bright side. The flashes of lightning will light the way for us."

"And my mother always told me not to stand under a tree during a thunderstorm."

We both laughed, then began running toward the finish line.

As expected, we found the second bridge uninhabited. After we crossed it and broke out into the clearing, we could see our friends waiting under one of the picnic shelters at the end of the road. Once our silhouettes were visible as we jogged down the middle of the street, we heard them cheering and watched them gather at the front of the structure. Thank goodness, Barb happened to have a couple of beach towels in her car!

"Wow, man – good going!" She smiled and tossed me a towel.

Everyone was anxious to hear about our adventure.

"What was it like?"

"Were you scared?"

"See any ghosts or witches?"

"Nope, it was a walk in the park!" We responded with large innocent smiles. "It was really cool!"

"God, your faces are all covered with mosquito bites!" one of the girls noticed.

We'd given up on fighting the flying blood suckers ten minutes after entering the woods, so this is something we expected.

Ironically, our clothes were already soaking wet even before the rains came. Nervous perspiration had flowed non-stop from every pore in our bodies making us smell sweaty and rank. Thank goodness the rain provided a cleansing shower!

"Hey, how come you guys are carrying clubs and all those big rocks?" someone asked, garnering the attention of those around us.

"Yeah, what's that all about?" demanded another.

Wayne and I looked at each other, 'Uh-oh... busted!'

SIXTEEN - LISTENING POST (0500 HOURS)

The rain stopped as suddenly as it began just minutes before the team's hourly sit-rep at 0500. It had temporarily vanquished the mosquitoes, so it was safe for the two soldiers to stick their heads out of their soaking wet cocoons.

If they had been able to see one another, both would have laughed hysterically at the other. Polack's boony hat was still on his head, but the wide circular brim had drooped, covering his face and ears, the bulky poncho liner, absorbing its dripping water. The camouflage stripes on his face were smeared and runny like a woman's mascara after crying. His teeth chattered as his body temperature dropped.

LG was a mirrored image of Polack except for his boony hat. After Sgt. Rock had jammed the hat over LG's ball of hair and forced the brim to jam around his forehead, LG left it that way all night. Now, the overstuffed hat was deflated and leaning to one side like a wet dish rag. He, too, suffered from the freezing temperature, his chattering teeth in sync with Polack's. Even the radio handset looked like it was vibrating against his ear.

The newly-formed lake within their shallow depression had disappeared; the thirsty ground wasted no time in absorbing the foot-deep water, leaving behind a muddy paste that would dry up and harden within a few hours.

Their light-weight poncho liners changed colors to a deeper forest green covered with brown caked mud. Soaking wet, the liners weighed almost fifteen pounds, but they would dry within a couple of hours. Meanwhile, it was all they had to help keep them warm.

Only thirty minutes more for this detail; both soldiers glanced at their watches, silently willing the minute hands to move faster.

They were facing east and could finally see the first rays of sunlight getting brighter and introducing a new day. The jungle began waking up: foliage stretched, trees grew another millimeter, and the resident creatures started croaking, chirping and singing to their mates.

As the light illuminated the ground, battleship gray and black silhouetted backgrounds changed into bright green, yellow and brown. A slight mist covered the ground, rising to a height of six feet. This hour was a critical part of the day, as enemy soldiers used the morning mist to conceal their movements and wreak havoc wherever possible. LG and Polack shimmied along the ground and scooted back into their depression, resuming their original positions, allowing the muddy bottom to provide a slight cushion for their sore tailbones. Only one of the three firing devices for the Claymores was still hot; LG brushed it off and then placed the other two worthless clackers off to the side. Meanwhile, Polack plucked the grenades from the mud. Using his hands and the wet liner, he cleaned them, rebent the pin ends and then set them on the rim of the depression to their front.

With fifteen minutes to go, the trail before them became visible as the mist evaporated. Both hoped that nobody crossed that trail; there'd been enough excitement for one night. LG and Polack were physically and emotionally spent after staying awake for most of the night; their fear of discovery and the very real possibility of dying during the night tapped into whatever reserve remained. Their imaginations in overdrive had caused most of the stress, but thankfully, the light of day chased those dreadful thoughts away.

LG crinkled his nose and pointed it straight into the air, his lips puckering with each deep sniff.

"I smell breakfast!"

Polack faced the sky and took several deep whiffs of his own.

"Smells like bacon and fresh coffee," he commented, the corners of his mouth turning upward in a half-smile.

"This is blowing my mind. What are we, a quarter mile or so from the firebase?"

Polack shook his head in agreement.

"Funny how that smell can overpower all the other funkiness in the air."

The guys began salivating over the wafting scents, smacking their lips in anticipation.

"I can taste it already!"

Their spirits lifted at the thought.

SEVENTEEN - RETURNING TO THE FIREBASE

At 0530, Polack left the depression and crawled forward through the thick brush to secure the remaining Claymore mine. He retracted the blasting cap and rolled up the wire onto a spool during his return. LG also pulled in his two wires and wrapped them around the clackers. Both leads were much shorter now with ragged tears at the ends from the explosions. They would come in handy out in the bush when setting up NDP's.

With everything packed, they were ready to leave this nightmare. LG called the CP,

"Thunder 3, Lima Papa 1, over."

"This is Thunder 3, go!"

"Roger, Lima Papa 1 is waiting for Alpha Romeo 6 and then returning to base with them."

He grabbed the ammo belt attached to the radio and hefted it onto his shoulder.

"Roger Lima Papa 1, will inform the perimeter. Welcome back! Thunder 3, out."

The radio operator's voice was different; LG suspected that he was the day shift replacement for the RTO who had kept them company during the night, and who was most likely already in line at the mess hall. The other three ambush and LP teams called in and were also returning to base.

Polack and LG struggled out of their hiding place and farther through the brush, finally reaching the trail. There, they saw the craters formed by the exploded Claymores and noted the extensive damage. The vegetation was blown to pieces, and many of the nearby tree trunks were missing bark and pocked with dozens of holes; some of the newer saplings were decapitated. *'No living creature or human being within thirty feet of these exploding mines could have survived or even remained whole,'* they thought.

Knowing that Rock's squad would soon be coming down the eastern trail, Polack and LG split and moved apart along the intersecting road to provide security for the group moving their way.

Five minutes later, Rock's ambush team arrived and stopped momentarily at the intersection until Polack and LG pulled back and joined them. Most everyone carried a second rifle - the AK-47 rifles slung over their shoulders - two carried NVA rucksacks, and two others struggled with the mortar plate and tripod.

"Vince," Sgt. Rock whispered, "give the mortar plate to LG, he can carry it back to the firebase." The skinny white kid smiled broadly and handed the dense baseplate to the surprised man.

'What the fuck is this all about?' LG thought, then joined the column in a procession to their home-away-from-home.

After about twenty steps, LG turned to Polack who was following behind him. "Do me a solid, Polack, and carry this radio. This plate got to weigh 25 pounds or more." LG held the 26-pound radio by the strap in his outstretched hand, his momentum swinging it like a pendulum. Polack reached out and accepted it freely without saying a word; he let the radio hang from his shoulder and rest against his hip.

"Rock's got it in for me," LG complained after glancing backward.

"I betcha it's your boony hat and that cool Afro of yours." Polack teased, trying his best to lighten the mood and cheer LG up. "I bet he's proud that you didn't mess with it after he form-fitted it to your head."

"I'm hip, my brother. But I'm still pissed, though. Now I've got to get a new hat, and it's gonna take me a couple of hours to comb out and reshape my 'do. The Bloods are gonna be all up in my case!"

"I hear ya'!" Polack agreed, chuckling at the thought of his bud catching hell over his hairstyle.

The column exited the jungle and once again crossed over the unstable bulldozed clearing, moving in a more relaxed manner at this point, straight to the concertina wire and bunkers of the firebase. All in all, the trip only took twenty minutes.

As they passed through the main gate, several of the soldiers manning the nearest bunker started laughing and pointing at the column of men. One of them shouted in a Southern drawl, "Hey man, which of you are the guys who played baseball with the apes last night?"

"Yeah, that must have been far out!" another added. "What was the final score?" The laughing and taunting continued.

LG and Polack hung their heads as they moved forward. Another voice called from the same bunker,

"I knew it, it was Polack and LG!" The laughter increased as the men began throwing small rocks toward the column, purposely landing short. "Come on batter, batter, sawwing!" someone hollered in mockery. Mystified, Polack and LG wondered how that bunch found out about their embarrassing experience so soon. When they looked up, everyone in Rock's group was pointing them out. Their fellow brothers had sold them out!

"Oh, great!" Polack declared. "That's some bogue shit!"

"Fuck it! Don't mean nothin'!" LG shook his head in dismay. "Those chumps would have spazzed out if they were in our place."

"Fuck all you guys!" Polack yelled and raised the middle finger of both hands toward the group on the perimeter.

"Yeah! And we won the ballgame!" LG added then joined Polack in the silent salute.

Those men atop the bunker continued hollering insults; their celebration became extremely animated and the laughter intense. One soldier stepped too close to the edge and fell off, landing on his back and getting the wind knocked out of him. The mishap created just enough diversion for Polack and LG to get away. Both knew the group was only blowing off steam. Now that the night had disappeared, it was their way of relieving the stress after living through a mortar attack and hearing those sounds of battle nearby. Only ten minutes more, and the daytime bunker guards would be replacing them.

Bunkers didn't have PRC-25 radios and weren't able to monitor the exchanges between their CP and those units in the bush. Most likely, they found out when the CP informed them with bits and pieces of information during the night.

Soon, the column stopped at the Battalion Command Bunker and began unloading the bounty from their ambush. The colonel and a few other officers exited the bunker and joined the group, congratulating them on their success. One by one, they began picking up the weapons and looking through the other confiscated supplies. At that point, Rock's squad started to split up, with some heading to their hooches and others to the mess tent. Sergeant Rock remained behind to answer more detailed questions.

Polack carried the radio into the CP bunker and checked it in with the RTO on duty. First Sergeant Hawkins happened to notice him and called out from behind his desk,

"Polack, is your partner, LG, still outside?" Top was a big man with a light brown crew-cut, black rimmed military glasses, and starched jungle fatigues with sharp creases on the arms and legs. He sat on an upturned ammo crate puffing on a fat cigar, its blue smoke rising to the ceiling and enshrouding him in a pale fog. He looked through a handful of papers, then set them down on the folding table, removed the cigar, and took a drink of steaming coffee from his canteen cup.

Alarmed by the sudden acknowledgment, the soldier stopped and turned to face the head NCO.

"Yeah, I think so, First-Sergeant.".

"Good, go and fetch him, and the two of you hurry back."

Polack walked through the sandbagged doorway and called over to LG. He had just dropped the mortar base plate next to the tripod in front of the bunker.

"Hey, partner!" LG looked his way. "Top wants to see us."

"Why?" LG asked, trying to straighten his boony hat.

"Not a clue. But come on, we better not keep him waiting."

The two men walked back into the bunker and stopped in front of the First Sergeant.

"What's up, Top?" Polack asked.

Sgt. Hawkins looked up once again from his paperwork, and after seeing LG standing there in his boony, a sudden twitch near his cheek pulled at the corners of his mouth to form a half smile.

"You boys get some chow and be ready to move out with your squads at 0900."

Both men responded simultaneously,

"Top, we just got back from spending the night out on LP. We're hungry and need to crash."

Top raised his hand for them to stop.

"I know where you've been and know that you're both tired. Join the rest of the crowd."

"But, Top," Polack began and stopped when Top raised a finger this time.

"The entire First Platoon is going out to sweep the area where Rock targeted the enemy mortar tube last night to poke around where they blew the ambush. The bodies may still be there, and there's a chance that Rock's group might have missed something in the dark. Sgt. Holmes will fill you in before leaving." He offered his sternest look to the men. "Dismissed!"

The two men stood in place, momentarily stunned at the news. Polack finally lightly swatted his partner on the hip,

"C'mon G, let get some chow."

Top went back to his stack of papers; the two men turned and walked out.

"This is bullshit! Them lifers got nothin' better to do than fuck with us, brothers…"

Polack interrupted LG,

"Wait a minute now, LG, I'm not black. So how is the man only fucking with the brothers? I'll be there walking right behind you on this patrol."

"Yeah, I know you ain't black, but you still a brother!"

Polack laughed at his statement.

"Shit ain't right, Polack, and I don't know about you, but last night was the most terrifying night of my life. I lost count of the number of times we shoulda' been killed."

LG hesitated while they got in line at the mess tent before continuing.

"First, the gook platoon almost stepped on us, and then the mortar fire and artillery rounds went off, Rock's ambush, and then them fucking apes messin' with us, and everybody else thinks it's funny!"

"I feel for ya, G, and I was just as freaked out! My asshole puckered up so tight; I won't be able to shit for a week!" Both men laughed to relieve the tension.

"You know, we can take our chow back to the hootch and try to catch some Z's after eating. We might luck out and get a little more than two hours before we have to leave."

"Yeah, you right!"

Upon reaching their hootch, Sergeant Holmes exited as Polack reached for the door. They all expressed surprise at seeing one another.

"Sgt. Holmes..." Polack didn't get a chance to finish.

"Can it, Polack! I don't want to hear your whining about this patrol. It is what it is, and there's nothing anybody can do about it. I have my orders, just like you have yours!"

LG and Polack were shocked for the second time in fifteen minutes.

"We weren't going to bitch about anything. We just wanted to say good morning to ya'," Polack recovered with a sly smile.

"Right on!" LG added wholeheartedly.

Sgt. Holmes looked confused momentarily, then broke into a grin.

"Why do I have to have all the smart asses in my platoon?" he asked, and then walked away shaking his head. He stopped and turned after several feet.

"Get some sack time, I'll wake ya's when it's time to go!"

Sgt. Holmes turned again and resumed his walk toward the mess tent.

Walking through the door, LG declared,

"Ya' know, Sarge ain't bad for a lifer. I sorta like the guy!"

"You got that right!" Polack agreed. He set his equipment to the side and then crashed, face first, onto his cot.

EPILOGUE

Life presents trials while growing up, periodically placing us in situations where we come face-to-face with fear. Hopefully, we learn from these experiences and then move forward. For me, running was often the response to fear during my adolescent years. Pure adrenaline propelled me to safety, and I'd never be able to match that same speed at any other time. As you mature, you look back at those earlier fears and scoff at how foolish they were. Life must have created a written script to follow, because most of us have faced similar fears and can relate to the comparable stories of others.

Fear of the unknown is a challenging sensation that we might experience at any age. In many cases, I can look back today and laugh at some of my childhood reactions, although they weren't funny at the time. However, fear continued to visit and make its presence known, and life regularly gave me new reasons to be afraid. My "fight-or-flight" reflex was frequently on overdrive.

I still have nightmares, but not because of dark basements, witches, or scary movies. (Oh, I take that back... one movie, 'The Exorcist', got the best of my wife and me.) Those new fears that I experience today are still because of the unknown, but they're of a completely different nature. As adults, our worst trepidations usually deal with serious issues such as having a first child, starting a new job, paying bills, divorce, purchasing a new home, encountering natural disasters, or illness, just to name a few. Of course, there are times when we'd all like to run away from our problems in life.

I firmly believe that dealing with the fears of my youth helped to shape the person I am today. At the same time, I sometimes marvel that events I experienced in my lifetime did not send me over the brink! Instead, my wife and daughter think of me as a person with a calm, passive demeanor... their hero... their rock. I guess I'm a pretty good actor.

#####

AUTHOR'S NOTE: GOOD LUCK CHARMS AND SUPERSTITIONS

When writing 'When Can I Stop Running?', it brought to mind many of the Alpha Company group discussions that took place at least once a month, either at a firebase or back in Cu Chi. The subject of good luck charms, superstitions, and religion was one of the most frequently debated. Most of the soldiers in Vietnam carried a talisman of some kind – an object believed to protect them from evil. These items became an important part of their daily lives. We were young and needed something to hang onto...something to give us hope...something to help keep our fears at bay...something to give us strength...something to help us get back home alive and in one piece after twelve months in Hell.

The most common of these amulets were religious items such as crosses hanging from chains, medallions of St. Christopher, scapulars, rosary beads, and bibles.

Many soldiers also carried pictures of their girlfriends or wives. Infantry soldiers usually kept them inside their helmets or within metal ammo cans that were stored under rucksacks. One man wore a piece of green yarn around his wrist, a gift from his two-year-old daughter upon leaving home. I also saw rabbit feet in various colors, unique coins, engraved lighters and small American flags. All were slices of home and cherished mementos.

Some soldiers wore vintage survival knives in sheathes or possessed other military keepsakes and heirlooms handed down through their families for generations. The Bowie knife one particular soldier carried saw service in World War II, Korea, and then the second of two tours in Vietnam; he was the fourth family member to wear it during a war.

Others kept tokens representing a "sign of the times" from back home - meant to make a statement rather than function as a good luck charm: peace symbols, "love" beads, and jewelry fashioned from braided boot laces. The latter - necklaces, wristbands, and pendants - represented "Black Power" and many African-American soldiers wore them to support that movement back in the world.

Personally, I fabricated a charm just before going out to the bush for the first time. I took a 50 caliber tracer round and separated the copper slug from its brass casing. Next, I lit the red incendiary powder, dug out the spent powder from within the copper bullet, looped some trip wire inside, then filled the empty cavity with a mixture of mud and concrete. Once dried, I threaded a simple chain through the hand made eyelet and wore it around my neck 24/7, never removing it until the day I left Vietnam. At the out-processing center in Cam Ranh Bay, I was stopped by MP's prior to boarding the Freedom Bird and told that I was not allowed to leave Vietnam with my good luck charm, and was forced to leave it in the contraband box.

What about superstitions? Many soldiers carried Ace of Spades playing cards with them while on patrol, then left them on dead enemy bodies or scattered them around the battlefield. Americans thought the cards scared or spooked enemy soldiers, but years later we heard that the symbol didn't impact them in the least. In retrospect, we can all agree the playing card, at a minimum, was a motivator and morale booster for those American troops.

Most of us have experienced premonitions of some sort during our lives. Some may refer to this phenomenon as their "sixth sense" kicking in. During the Vietnam war, any number of things may have triggered that overwhelming and inexplicable feeling of dread. It may have been something in the air that just didn't smell right, noticing the sudden silence of the jungle, or hearing an unfamiliar sound. Those gut feelings that something catastrophic was about to happen were experienced by enlisted men, officers, short-timers, and Cherries alike. Many times there was no explanation for the sudden stab of foreboding and fear the soldiers experienced; most likely it was all a part of their survival instinct. Failure to act on these "warnings" often had disastrous – and sometimes fatal – results. Yet there were those who chalked up acting on those cautionary apprehensions as superstition.

Many troops heavily smoked cigarettes, and, of course, most everyone carried lighters. C-Rations meals included matches, but they were useless during the monsoon season. Soldiers had their Zippo lighters engraved with a variety of slogans and acronyms; many being personal messages or a dedication to someone back home. Lighters carried in the breast pocket of a fatigue jacket had been known to stop a bullet otherwise destined for a soldier's chest.

One superstition involved the lighting of three cigarettes from a single match. When more than two soldiers required a light, a new match was struck after the second cigarette

175

was lit. To vary that routine in any way was considered a sure harbinger of misfortune.

One man I served with stored a six-pack of beer along with his personal belongings in the rear area storage connex upon his arrival in-country. It was his second tour, but he considered this six-pack his lucky charm - something to savor after surviving twelve more months in-country. Unfortunately, after transferring to another unit, someone raided his duffel bag and pilfered his "special talisman". Subsequently, on his first mission after eight months in-country, he tripped a booby trap and tragically lost both of his legs. Coincidence, or not?

The mountain people of Vietnam, referred to as Montagnards, hated the VC and NVA soldiers, and the ARVN who discriminated against them and bullied them. They were great fighters, but a superstitious lot. Many of them treasured simple items such as stones, or pieces of wood and metal, revering them as talisman. Items hung from their necks, ears and waists, but those dangling items made a lot of noise when humping through the jungle. A story was told of a Green Beret adviser, who, early in the war, ordered all those tribesmen on the mission with him to leave their noisy charms behind. Reluctantly, they complied with the order. Later in the mission, this same patrol walked into an enemy ambush and lost most of their troops, along with the SF advisor. You can guess how this event was perceived back in the village, and then how the account was passed on to others.

It was difficult to debate religion; most everyone believed that their faith in a God would protect them from evil. Many did not want to take sides when the Catholics, Baptists, and Lutherans argued over which was the true religion. However, there were always proclaimed atheists in every group; many had the fortitude to stand up and take on everybody else. They usually didn't last long in those debates before the group expelled them. The next day, all was forgiven, and everybody reunited with their brothers-in-arms. Most of us fervently believed that there was no such thing as an atheist in a foxhole during a fire-fight. In fact, this was the time that God received bunches of new recruits and promises to never miss a future church service or elude the donation plate.

Many argued that luck had nothing to do with their survival, and instead attributed their successes to training and overcoming fear.

As a final comment about luck and survival: During my year in Vietnam, I evaded the Reaper on four different occasions; each should have resulted in my untimely death. I tripped two booby traps; one failed to detonate, and the other resulted in only minor shrapnel wounds to my arm. I tripped the wire of an American mechanical ambush with four Claymore mines; enemy soldiers had discovered it earlier and removed the blasting cap, then forgot to re-arm it before leaving the area. I survived a bite from a highly poisonous Banded Krait snake. Finally, when walking point, I watched an enemy soldier shoot directly at me from a short distance away and he very fortunately missed me. An answer to prayer? Karma? Luck from my talisman? Good training? That will depend on who is answering that question!

Dear Reader

Thank you for taking the time to read *When Can I Stop Running?*. Please consider taking a moment to leave an honest review on the site where you made the purchase. It need not be long - even the short reviews are appreciated and add to the book's success.

After publishing my first book, *Cherries – A Vietnam War Story*, I set up a website where readers can leave comments, questions, and then view my personal photos from the war. Since then, it's evolved into a site that many say is filled with a wealth of history about the Vietnam War. Visitors can access more than 200 articles, videos, photos, songs, and slang terms used during the Vietnam war era. Many attest that this website has been very educational, as new and returning visitors continue to learn about the conflict and its warriors. New articles are posted weekly. I will use this website for both of my books, and I welcome your feedback. Please take a moment to visit when you can (see address below).

http://cherrieswriter.com/

ABOUT THE AUTHOR

John Podlaski served in Vietnam during 1970 and 1971 as an infantryman with both the Wolfhounds of the 25th Division and the 501st Infantry Brigade of the 101st Airborne Division. He was awarded the Combat Infantry Badge, Bronze Star, two Air Medals, and a Vietnamese Cross of Gallantry. He has spent the years since Vietnam working in various management positions within the automotive industry, and he recently received his Bachelor of Science degree in Business Administration. John is a life member of Vietnam Veterans of America Chapter 154. John and his wife, Jan, are both retired now and live in Sterling Heights, Michigan where they occasionally ride his Harley Davidson motorcycle.

Other books by this author:

Cherries: A Vietnam War Novel: This is a painfully accurate description of the life of a combat infantryman serving in the jungles of Vietnam. It portrays, in sometimes chilling detail, the swings he experienced between stifling boredom and utter terror that made up the life of this often-unappreciated soldier. The narrative is compelling, and the storytelling is excellent throughout. If you want to know what these young and not so young men saw and felt, this will help you gain a bit of understanding of the sacrifices they made.

The e-book version remained within the top 100 of the Amazon Top Seller lists in its category since its inception in 2010.

On January 21, 2013, PageOneLit dot com named *Cherries - A Vietnam War Novel* by John Podlaski - _BEST AUDIOBOOK OF 2012._ This was a proud moment for John Podlaski - recipient of the *"Books and Authors Award for Literary Excellence".*

When notified by contest officials of his good fortune in winning the audiobook category, the e-mail included the following quote from one of the contest judges, **"One HELL of a book!!!"**

Find it here: https://www.amazon.com/Cherries-Vietnam-Novel-John-Podlaski-ebook/dp/B003R4Z5U6

Unhinged – A Micro Read: Two fourteen-year-old boys are offered a great first-time opportunity to watch a movie by themselves at a local drive-in theater. Little did they realize that the movie would affect them in ways neither imagined nor will ever forget.

Find it here:

https://www.amazon.com/Unhinged-Micro-Read-John-Podlaski-ebook/dp/B089LGHPZJ

Unwelcomed: **A Short Story** - John Kowalski makes it home from the Vietnam War in one piece, and his battles are finally over. Or so he thought. Home for less than a week, John must defend his family from a pair of unwelcomed thugs hell-bent on revenge.

Find it here:

https://www.amazon.com/dp/B08GY46XGZ

Death in the Triangle: DEATH IN THE TRIANGLE is a sequel to "When Can I Stop Running?". That was one hell of a night!

Only a couple of hours passed since returning to the firebase, now, the sleep deprived, and weary First Platoon soldiers must go back out on another patrol. Last night, an enemy mortar team fired several rounds into the base and was soon silenced by return artillery fire. The Third Squad also ambushed a group of enemy soldiers leaving nine dead bodies on the trail before moving out to a new location. A thorough search of both areas may locate items overlooked in the dark. It was thought to be an easy patrol – two clicks out and two clicks back, so the brass expected their return before lunch. At least, that was the plan.

Many patrols during the Vietnam War did not quite go as planned and this was one of them. These soldiers soon found themselves in dire straits to satisfy their battalion commander's thirst for body counts and fame. Will they all survive?

Sixpack, Polack, LG, and the bunch are back in this new installment from the award-winning author of "Cherries: A Vietnam War Novel."

Find it here:

https://www.amazon.com/Death-Triangle-Vietnam-War-Story-ebook/dp/B096R3TTMD

Made in United States
Orlando, FL
30 May 2022

18332209R00100